THE OUTCAST OF CHIVASSO

WITNESSES OF THE LIGHT

The OUTCAST of CHIVASSO

a novella of the Waldensians

D. J. Speckhals

All rights reserved. Published in the United States by Locust Lamp Press, Pennsylvania, United States of America
www.djspeckhals.com

Trade Paperback edition ISBN: 978-1-7375364-5-1

eBook ISBN: 978-1-7375364-4-4

Front cover artwork: *Praying Girl* by Roberto Ferruzzi, Public domain
Back cover artwork: *Winter Landscape With Skaters* by Fredrik Marinus Kruseman, Public domain

Author photograph by: Following Splendor Images

1 3 5 7 9 10 8 6 4 2

First Edition

To my daughters—

Aliza and Emma

1

Praise ye the LORD. Praise the LORD, O my soul.

—Psalm 146:1

Late winter 1445

EVERY STEP ON the snow-covered road took more of what little life remained in Raimond Durand. The wind bit his hands, his forehead, and the slivers of skin exposed through the holes in his breeches. A gust blew in from the left and pushed him into a snowdrift for the third time that evening.

He closed his eyes and panted. The snow and wind would not defeat him.

Raimond coughed against the wind, and more warmth fled from his body. He reached into his coat pocket and felt for the one thing he could never lose. *Still there by my heart, exactly where it always is.*

He forced himself up from the snow, grabbed his hat, and gazed through the swirling torment. Somewhere beyond this weather was his place of refuge, where at last he could rest his legs, cast off his tattered clothing for something fresh, and sit with his feet propped up near a crackling hearth. If the Lord willed it, he would enter Valle di Luserna in two days, and there he could gather strength for the next adventure.

But he must find shelter tonight, or the last thing he might see would be icy blackness. Raimond trudged onward through the gusts, onward through the frozen wastelands of Piedmont, and onward through the heartaches that tempted him toward despair.

Up ahead, a stone wall materialized, then a house with a chimney spewing sparks and ashes. He dared not ask for shelter, for no friends dwelled between here and the Luserna Valley. Time and experience had taught him he could trust no one, not even a smiling child. Anyone could tell the local clergy who he was, where he traveled, or, worse, what he preached.

The only sound was the snow creaking and crunching under his feet. Raimond passed one house, then another, until a village of stone houses rose around him. Towering over all was the village cathedral. Its brick facade featured a portal flanked by multiple arches below a rose window with delicate tracery. Dominating the roofline was a series of steeply pitched gables along with sculptures depicting angels and saints. A torch lit the bell tower and cast an eerie glow over the village.

By his reckoning, this was the village of Chivasso, the last place of any size before Turin. Compared to the richer lands he had come from, these northwestern reaches of Italy were bare and uncivilized. Yet God had made a small corner of them a refuge for Raimond and many others like him—an ark for the faithful.

As he neared the village square, he pressed his back against the stone wall of the cathedral, hoping to gain a brief respite from the tempests. *I don't want to stay here long.*

To the left, an eight-sided tower guarded the sleepy village, and on the right, a set of wooden stocks stood before the cathedral's portal, awaiting their next victim. He crept under the shadow of the cathedral until the stocks also shadowed him.

A door creaked open on the far side of the square. A rotund woman stumbled out, put her hands on her head, and spit into the air. Raimond ducked and hid behind the stocks. No one must see him wandering through the village. Suspicions would arise, rumors would fester, and before he could plan an escape, his feet would be bound in the stocks he now leaned against.

The woman walked toward the cathedral and squinted in his direction. Raimond straightened his back and held his breath. *Lord, You've protected me for five years. Keep me safe under Your shadow.*

A hack echoed through the square again, then another creak and the slam of a door.

Raimond dropped his shoulders and let his breath escape. His fingertips no longer ached from the cold, but numbness was worse than pain, for that meant frostbite was setting in.

As fast as his tired limbs allowed, he left Chivasso and soon came upon a riverbank—the mighty River Po, if his memory served him. A small villa stood along the road to the right, and beyond that, a barn. Perhaps there he could find a few moments of rest among the animals and, if God blessed, a handful of grain to eat. If there were no cows needing to be milked, he might sleep past sunrise—much later than usual, but needed.

Raimond shielded his face from the wind with his right hand and crept toward the barn, watching for signs of human life. Finding none, he took careful steps to the door, raised the latch, and pressed on the dry-rotted wood. He cringed and waited for the door to creak, but it didn't, and neither did a cow moo. He peered in, but all was murky black.

A bleat rattled through the barn. Raimond tensed and gripped the doorframe, then sighed in relief.

He squeezed through the open door, shut it, and stooped down. He closed his eyes, useless in this dark place anyway, and let his other senses take over. The musty, earthy scent along with the bleats coming from different directions revealed its occupants. If it was a sheep barn, there would be straw for bedding. God had provided far more than Raimond deserved.

He crawled farther inside, not caring what barn-floor delicacies would find their way onto his palms and knees. Yet the floor was surprisingly clean. After a moment of crawling and feeling, Raimond found a mound of loose straw. He pushed his hands into the stack, making sure no other creatures had made it their home, spread the straw across the floor, and nestled in. He still shivered, but finally no incessant wind haunted his ears, and no snow pelted his eyes. He removed his tattered hat and swept away the snow from what remained of his coat, then pressed his hands against his beard to thaw the ice crystals. At first his fingertips tingled, but the tingling soon became a stinging pain. He rolled around as much as his muscles could endure and rubbed his hands together to dull the pain.

Yet when the cold pains subsided, the hunger pangs intensified. These weren't new pains, though. His hungry nights as a boy on the streets of Chambéry had formed him, but they also made him thankful for the abundance he often experienced now.

Raimond reached into his pocket and felt for his last morsel of bread, but stopped. Two days of walking remained, and he needed strength. He could wait until tomorrow. At last he closed his eyes.

A feathery touch drifted across his cheek. He pushed away the straw, but it wasn't straw.

He jumped at the feel of a cold nose and whiskers. The cat purred in his ear, begging to be petted. Somewhere between asleep and awake, Raimond rubbed the cat's back until it curled up against his chest and fell asleep with him. *Thank You, Lord, for each one of Your creatures.*

2

While I live will I praise the Lord: I will sing praises unto my God while I have any being.

—Psalm 146:2

A RUSTLING NOISE STARTLED Raimond awake. The wind had ceased, and the moon now cast a gentle light through a window high above.

The sound came again, this time from the shadows on the far side of the barn. Raimond bolted upright. The moonlight flickered as a human shape blocked it.

The cat rubbed its cheek on Raimond's coat, seemingly undisturbed by the intruder.

No, I'm the intruder.

Raimond extended his hand in apology. "*Mi scusa*," he said in the local Piedmontese dialect.

The figure moved but didn't retreat.

"I'll leave now." Raimond stood and slung his sack over his shoulder but kept his hand out. "I didn't steal or disturb anything."

A patting sound came from the person, then a whisper. "Come to me, Rosmarin."

That was the voice of a girl—a very young one.

The cat bounded toward the girl and leaped into her arms.

Raimond's heart raced. Her parents might be nearby, and she might tell them about the intruder in the barn. He had to be far away before she told them. He lowered his extended arm and turned to leave.

The girl flinched, but in doing so, she stepped into the moonlight. The hollow cheeks and drooping eyes told him everything, but her frail, trembling figure made Raimond's heart sink.

He glanced at his hands and clothing. Despite owning nothing save the few items in his sack and the clothes on his back, he was fat and rich compared to this feeble child. How old could she be? Perhaps six. By now Azalaïs would have been the same age, had not she and Maria—

Raimond drew in a breath as he felt for the tiny wooden box hidden in the pocket over his chest. After he was sure it was there, he reached into his other pocket for the hunk of stale bread. Though it was barely fit for a peasant, it might bring a smile to the girl's face. And she needed it far more than he did. "For you, *tòta. Pan.*" He smiled with one side of his mouth and gave a quick nod toward the bread.

Petting the cat but still trembling, the girl glanced at the bread before taking a hesitant step forward.

Raimond moved to meet her and softened his tone. "*Sì*, it's yours. There's nothing to fear from me, *cita.* I've been hungry before too, and I know what it feels like."

The girl's eyes widened as she took a step backward and held the cat tight. She turned and bolted to the other side of the barn.

Raimond felt his coarse, unkempt beard and windburned cheeks. In a dark place like this, he must look like a nightmare-worthy miscreant. Maria would have told him to wash up weeks ago.

The girl ducked through a gap in the wall, but the cat leaped from her arms. The sheep bleated when the cat pranced past them with its tail flung upward.

"Rosmarin, no." The girl backed out of the gap in the wall, turned, and patted her leg as if it were a drum. "Come to me, Rosmarin."

The cat ignored her, prancing its way toward Raimond, nestling up to his leg, and purring. Raimond crouched and petted the cat, watching the girl to see if she would return.

She kept her head down as she took timid steps toward Raimond.

"Rosmarin." Raimond scratched the cat under its chin, examining the dark stripes that flowed over its tan coat. "She's *fiamen-*

ga—very beautiful. Her fur kept me quite warm last night. Thank you for letting her sleep by me." He held the cat up and looked into its eyes. "And see here, God even gave her a fleur-de-lis over her nose and eyes."

The girl remained expressionless but continued to creep forward. Her hair was a frizzy, matted nest, likely filled with all manner of tiny creatures.

Raimond held out the bread again, and before he could blink, it was gone. The girl puffed out her cheeks like a hungry squirrel, so much so that she struggled to chew.

"Don't choke on it. Do you see anyone else I can give it to?"

The girl darted her eyes from side to side before looking back at Rosmarin, then Raimond. Above her stuffed mouth and gaunt cheeks, signs of warmth seeped into her eyes, and when she'd swallowed the last crumb, she gave him the most subtle of smiles.

Raimond tilted his head. "I'm sorry, that was my last piece."

The girl stooped over and rubbed behind Rosmarin's ears. "I found her in the summer, and now she's my friend."

"She's a good friend, I can see." Raimond stood, placed his hands on his hips, and glanced up at the window. "The sun will rise soon, and I must leave."

The girl pursed her lips. "Why did you sleep in here?"

"I'm walking home after a very long journey, and this barn seemed a warm and comfortable place for a bit of rest." Raimond eyed the girl. "Do you live here?"

"*Nò.*" She stirred the straw on the floor with her foot. "But I sometimes sleep here." She gave a slight wave and led him to the opposite side of the barn, where she stopped and pointed at a weathered wool coat and a necklace strung with bones, pebbles, and dried flowers. "*Babbo* gave these to me. Do you like them?"

"Euh, I suppose so." Raimond held up the necklace, probably the most her peasant father could afford.

"Babbo died in a war. *Mima* died when I was little."

Raimond's throat tightened, but he hid his sorrow. This poor child needed his empathy, but she needed his strength more. "Who cares for you now?"

"My *magna*, Babbo's sister. She lives in the village square by the cathedral. When Babbo left, he told me to stay with Magna until he returned. But he's not coming back now." The girl's face tightened, and a tear fell to the floor.

"Though it was many years ago, I lost my father and mother too."

"You're an orphan? You look like one."

Raimond cracked the slightest of smiles. "I suppose I was—or am—an orphan. But it's better not to dwell on such things. I try to grow in the strength of Christ instead."

The girl picked up the cat and slid her hand from the cat's head to the tip of its tail. "Do you hear her purring? She likes you, *monsù*."

Raimond scratched the cat behind its ears. "She likes all the attention too."

"We should be *amis*."

"If we're to be friends before I leave, we should know each other's names. *Mi im ës-ciamo* Monsù Raimond Durand. *Com it ës-ciame*?"

"Magna just calls me *maraja*, and everyone else started calling me that too."

Raimond squinted and shook his head. "She calls you a brat?"

"She's not a nice magna."

"Now what name did your babbo and mima give you?"

"Elionor!" A ray of light shone from the girl's face, brighter than the rising sun.

"Elionor—a name for a princess. That name suits you much better than *maraja*, so that's what I'll call you if you wish, and the three of us will be friends—you, me, and Rosmarin."

Elionor showed her teeth in a wide grin. "Sì, I like that." She set the cat on the ground and examined Raimond from his hat to his boots. "Monsù Raimond, where did you go on your journey?"

Raimond brushed straw and dirt from his coat. "My travels took me to the north, far away from here. Every spring, men like me—"

He caught himself. He didn't know this girl and couldn't trust her with his secrets. "I visit many villages and . . ." He glanced toward the door. "I'm sorry, I truly should leave."

"Are you a troubadour? I've never heard one, but my babbo told me about them."

"Nò, I'm not a troubadour. I enjoy singing, but not those kinds of songs."

"Then who are you? You talk a little funny."

As innocent as Elionor might seem, he couldn't trust her with that information—not in a place like Chivasso. He couldn't be too evasive, though, and she deserved to know something. Motioning for Elionor to follow, he walked to the door and opened it. A brood of hens pecked at the few blades of grass sticking through the snow, and behind a short fence, three hogs rooted in the slushy mud. To the left, the sun peeked over the horizon, and straight ahead, a cobblestone bridge arched over the River Po. The morning air chilled his skin, but at least the gales had eased.

Raimond knelt beside Elionor and pointed toward the horizon. "Just above the trees there, do you see those snowy mountains?"

Elionor squinted. "I think so."

"Below those mountains, in a valley you can't see from here— that's where my home is. My talking sounds different from yours because we speak a different language in that land. Some of us, men like me, leave the valley when the snow melts and travel to lands near and far."

"What do you do there?"

Raimond had already said too much. He chose his next words carefully. "That is a question I cannot answer, for there are some who hate what we do."

A light breeze swept past them. Raimond wrapped his coat tight around his chest and pulled down his hat. "*Mi amis* Elionor, it was a joy to meet you this morning, but I should return to my home before another snowstorm finds me."

"Your wife and children will be happy to see you."

A shadow fell over Raimond's soul. How pleasant it would have been to return to his wife and daughter—lovely Maria and her gentle, reassuring voice. And Azalaïs. How might she have looked after these six years?

"Once I had a wife and a daughter." Raimond's throat tightened. "My daughter would have been the same age as you."

"Seven?"

"Nearly. My wife—her name was Maria, and she was everything to me and more. We were so excited about having a child, but when the baby came, Maria was too weak." Raimond's voice cracked as he gazed toward the horizon again. He swallowed and straightened his shoulders. *I must be strong for this girl.* "Now God has given me a much larger family—not a wife and children, but friends sprinkled throughout this realm and others. He has given me far more than I deserve, and I see loving families in my valley every day I'm there."

"Families?" Elionor said, her eyes begging for more.

"I know many wonderful families." Janavels, Orsellos, Pavarins, and more, but those names would mean nothing to Elionor. "Truly, there is much I could say, but I doubt it would interest you."

"I don't think I've ever seen a wonderful family." Elionor dropped her gaze to the ground. "Magna says Mima left me and Babbo when I was a baby. Then Mima died. Magna is my family now, but she's not wonderful. She doesn't love me either. She says so."

"Surely your magna loves you." Raimond touched Elionor's hair but quickly drew his hand back. He didn't want those lice in his hair or beard. Her clothes were soiled and worn, her skin blotched, and she was starving. However much Elionor's aunt loved her, it wasn't enough. "Why does she make you sleep in this barn?"

"She doesn't know I sleep here, and she doesn't care as long as I'm not in her house those nights."

"But some nights you sleep in the house?"

"When I bring my ducats home for her. And when she's had too much to drink. She sleeps a long time when she's drunk, so I come to her house after dark and sleep by the hearth, and before she wakes up, I come back here to work. I clean the stalls, sweep the floor, and give the sheep, pigs, and chickens food and water."

"Do you work here every day?"

"Sì, and on the last day of the month, Ago gives me three ducats. He's the servant, but this is Monsù Damiano's barn, and the animals are his." Elionor frowned and pointed past the barn toward a stone house covered in moss. "Monsù Damiano lives up there, but I've never seen him. No one has. The older boys in the village say his hair is green and his eyes are red. He breathes fire like a dragon too.

Magna says he's as mean as a hornet in November, so she said I can never speak to him. Never."

Raimond raised his brows. "I'm more concerned about how this Monsù Damiano pays you. Surely you deserve more than three ducats a month."

Elionor stepped toward the barn. "I should start my work before Ago sees me doing nothing."

Raimond peered toward the mountains. Their silhouette was so faint that most people would mistake them for fog. The mountains were calling him, and once home in the valley, he could again dwell together in unity with brothers and sisters in Christ. This winter's journey might not have been as fruitful as others, but so it was sometimes. Few had listened to the gospel, and fewer had responded to it. But despite the setbacks, the Holy Scriptures were still effective, and the Holy Spirit still converted souls.

The cat meowed from inside the barn, and Raimond glanced in that direction.

"Rosmarin is saying she caught a mouse," Elionor said. "Do you want to see it?"

"I'm so hungry I could almost eat it."

"Not me! I don't eat mice!" Elionor's eyes sparkled in the dawn light, and her sweet demeanor could have melted a glacier. She might need a bath or three, but she was a girl whom God loved. She deserved better than what she had been forced into, more than what her life offered.

If she were a girl from his valley, a girl like Azalaïs, she would be working in the fields, milking the goats, helping her mother spin wool. In the evenings, she would study the Holy Scriptures and answer questions from the old catechisms of their faith, and she would be in a family—a family not only to feed her but also to listen to her fears, her doubts, and her dreams.

Raimond and Maria had prayed for a daughter. God had answered that prayer and given them one, but only for a vanishing moment. It all felt so long ago, but the pit left by Maria and Azalaïs remained.

Raimond glanced at the ground, then back at Elionor. If he

worked in another profession, and if he didn't look like a mountain vagrant, he would take Elionor from this place, rent a small plot in the valley, and give her the home she needed.

Elionor stepped toward Raimond and stood at his side, examining the ground with him. "What are you looking at, Monsù Raimond?"

Raimond shook off his unrealistic dreams and forced a grin. "I'm sorry, I often find myself lost in old memories." He turned toward the barn and offered Elionor his hand. "I will help you clean the barn today, and after we finish, I'll find my road home again."

Elionor hesitated, then took Raimond's hand and, with a slight hop in her step, led him to the barn. "The chickens lay less when it's cold, but Ago says Monsù Damiano eats four eggs every day before he goes to sleep. Ago is very cruel when I can't find four eggs."

Raimond grabbed a pitchfork, picked up a load of straw, and threw it into the sheep pen. Rosmarin lay in a nearby corner, watching Raimond refresh the sheep's bedding while Elionor searched for eggs. Even though Elionor was a famished seven-year-old girl, she had kept the barn quite clean. This place must have been a type of refuge for her—a place she could make to her liking despite the turmoil and uncertainty elsewhere. Raimond had found similar places when he was a boy.

"Do you enjoy working in this barn?" Raimond asked.

At first Elionor seemed as if she hadn't heard, but after a few moments of silence, she placed her basket of eggs on the floor and shrugged. "Magna says it's the best I could ask for, but I want to stay home like the other girls in the village. I don't have to work here past Easter, though."

"What's after Easter?"

"Magna says I'll be warmer and be able to eat more if I work at the tavern in the town square. If I clean there every morning, I'll get more than three ducats."

Raimond tossed his pitchfork aside. "Your magna wants you to work in a tavern? A seven-year-old girl?"

"What's bad about a tavern? All the people will be gone or asleep in the morning. Magna says that place gives her more joy than home and heaven."

"Your magna, what's her name?"

"Her friends call her Norma."

"This Norma . . ." Raimond's blood simmered, but he held his anger in. "She doesn't feed you. She doesn't let you sleep in the house. She makes you work in a filthy barn."

"It's not filthy, and I have Rosmarin, a bed, and all the animals. I clean the stalls, and I can eat whatever the animals don't."

"No longer." Raimond picked up Elionor's egg basket and gave her a firm look. "Elionor, you must listen to me. You ought to respect your magna, but you cannot work at the tavern."

"I don't want to, but I'm afraid. I don't want to make her un-happy with me again. Last time . . . last time . . ." Elionor wept.

Raimond bent down and let her bury her head in his shoulder. How did this girl pluck the strings of his heart so easily? No one else could do that. Was it because of Azalaïs? He could never resurrect that tiny body from the grave, but perhaps he and Elionor could help one another.

The powerful odor of Elionor's hair drifted into Raimond's nos-trils, but instead of recoiling in disgust, he hugged the girl tighter. Tears welled up in his eyes, but he refused to let them flow. Elionor needed more than his sympathy. She needed his aid.

When Elionor stopped crying, Raimond held her at arm's length and wiped a tear from her face. "I need to meet your magna. You shouldn't be working in that tavern."

"She doesn't like it when I come to her without asking first. She'll still be asleep. Or drinking. Magna drinks everything, and whenever she can't drink, she eats."

Raimond tried to hold back his grin but probably failed. He took Elionor's hand and marched through the barn door. "I'll speak to her. I have yet to meet a brutish woman whom I can't convince with a healthy mix of tact and boldness."

Elionor looked up with a blank expression. "You haven't met Magna."

3

Put not your trust in princes, nor in the son of man, in whom there is no help.

—Psalm 146:3

As the sun began its descent into the west, Raimond and Elionor entered the village square, where merchants at four or five stalls sold their goods in the open air despite the cold. The cathedral bells rang for midday prayers, but the villagers walking about the streets of Chivasso continued with the day's activities. In the shadows of the nearest stall, a gang of boys pointed across the way at a sleeping vendor who might soon wake and find himself with fewer wineskins than when he first rested his eyelids. A minstrel sat on a barrel and plucked the strings of a lute as he sang a melody in an old Romaunt dialect few spoke except in the narrow valleys and mountain slopes Raimond called home.

Among his people, he could speak freely about heavenly matters without the fear of someone telling a priest or, worse, an inquisitor. In places with ancient names like Luserna, Chisone, Rorà, and Angrogna, he could again sing and pray with people who believed as he did. Their small congregations might not gather in grand cathedrals like the one now towering before Raimond and Elionor, but where they met, they worshipped God according to the Holy Scriptures. Raimond could almost hear the sweet voices over the lute and the cathedral bells.

Elionor tugged on his hand, lifted a thin arm, and pointed an unsteady finger at a sign to the left. "The tavern."

But the sign did not say "The Tavern." Instead, a few crudely written words made him take a step back and forget the lute and bells.

"What happened, Monsù?" Elionor asked. "You look like you're in the sauce."

"In the sauce?"

"Sì, in the sauce."

Raimond crossed his arms and stared at Elionor.

"It means euh . . ." Elionor squinted at him. "I don't know how to say it."

"Do I look frightened? Guilty?"

"Maybe, but that's not what 'in the sauce' means. The sauce is bad."

"I understand now." He let out a restrained laugh. "You Piedmontese and your idioms. 'In the sauce' means 'in trouble.'"

"Sì, and we also say 'finish in the sauce.' And that means—"

"'Heading into trouble.'" Raimond lowered his voice and eyed the sign. "Exactly as we are now."

"It's only Magna. She's cruel, but she won't hurt you."

"Your magna doesn't concern me. It's what that sign says."

"'The Tavern'?"

"That may be what it is, but that sign doesn't say 'The Tavern.'"

Elionor shrugged. "What does it say?"

Raimond read the sign in a whisper. "'L'Erétich Ch'a Brusa.'" He grabbed Elionor's hand and turned away from the establishment. "It says THE BURNING HERETIC."

"I've heard Magna say that. What does it mean?"

The Piedmontese often constructed comic words or ironic phrases when they named their taverns and shops, but these words were like a basket overflowing with asps—only entertaining until they escaped.

"Don't concern yourself about it other than to know I won't allow a single one of your toes into that den of weasels."

Elionor gripped Raimond's hand tighter as they walked away from the tavern, and he squeezed back. Across the square, a man leaned against a wagon, whittling away at a stick, but he wasn't focused on the stick. Raimond tried to evade the man's gaze, but when he glanced back, it followed him and Elionor. Men and women both examined him, and the only way he avoided their curious eyes was by periodically observing the blue sky. Chivasso wasn't the friendly village it advertised itself to be, and he needed to leave it as soon as he spoke to this Norma.

After a hurried walk, they stood before an old timber door. Elionor scratched her head and looked up at Raimond. "Rosmarin hisses whenever she sees Magna, and Magna hisses back. When Magna yells, I look at the ground. That way I don't smell her breath or feel her spit on my face."

Raimond knocked and prepared to leverage Elionor's advice.

The hinges squealed like trapped rabbits as the door opened no wider than Raimond's hand. A gruff but still womanly voice leaped from the crack. "What's your business?"

Standing straight and spreading his feet, Raimond wrapped his right hand around the edge of the door and pressed. The woman slammed the door before Raimond could pull away his fingers. He bit his lip and winced as a sharp pain shot up his right arm. Again he knocked, this time with his left hand, and raised his voice. "Norma, I'm here for your niece."

The door flung open, and a laugh bellowed out from inside the house. " 'Stay three steps back from the mule's *darera*,' they say. Next time don't invite yourself into my house."

Raimond almost glanced away. The woman's graying blonde hair fell from her very round head like lengths of greasy old rope. Beneath her low brow, two scalding brown eyes stared into his being.

"This is Magna." Elionor's voice quivered.

Raimond straightened his back but refused to bow. He was a commoner, she was a commoner, and this wasn't the place for formality. "I am Raimond Durand."

Norma hacked something up from deep in her throat. "Who's this?"

"My friend." Elionor slunk behind Raimond and held on to a leg of his breeches.

Raimond narrowed his eyes and stared at Norma. "Do you see how hungry she is? Or her hair? And you make her sleep in a barn?"

"*Darmagi*, the poor, innocent maraja." Norma formed her lower lip into a pout and pretended to weep, then spat on the toe of Raimond's boot. "And you—the man who dreams he's Saint Joseph himself, ready to strike me down at my own house." She took a step forward and jutted her jaw up at Raimond. "What are you going to do, Saint Joseph?"

Precisely as Elionor had warned, Norma's breath made Raimond flinch. "I'm no saint, *Madama*." He had to cough out that last word. "Far from it. I'm but a lone traveler who happened upon a hungry, unkept, and unloved girl whose name is Elionor, not maraja."

"Saint Joseph." Norma breathed hard into Raimond's nostrils. "You like that name, don't you? I will say, you're right about one thing. No one loves the maraja. Her filthy mima, Gisella, died in her own vomit, and her fool of a babbo heaved her onto my lap when he left on some quest for the pope. Then he died. Sì, I wept. Can you imagine that?" She scratched behind her ear. "I loved my brother and all he stood for, but then he left his little *cucciola* for me to feed and groom."

"Which you haven't bothered to do."

Norma tightened her lips. "Since you're such a saintly saint, why don't you feed her? See, I know why you don't answer me. You are nothing, and you have nothing, so you want to lay your guilt on me, blaming the girl's pitiful magna instead of your own filth and poverty."

Raimond's skin tingled. This vile woman wasn't worth the words he'd already spent on her, but Elionor was. Raimond cleared his throat. "You don't know me."

"I do now, and *mersì* for not making yourself known to me sooner. But since you stand there, I welcome you to Chivasso of Piedmont, where no man keeps a wife, where no child obeys her elder"—she scowled at Elionor—"and where no woman is required to listen to a vagrant on the doorstep of her house. *Adiù*, and begone with you."

Norma took a step toward the door. Raimond stepped into her path and faced her. "I came to this house in all cordiality. I came to tell you that Elionor should not work in the tavern and that you should feed her. But now I've seen and smelled what I expected. Elionor, sì, *Elionor*, needs a family with no connection to you."

Norma threw her head back and cackled. "I beg you, Saint Joseph, take her from me. I'll light a thousand candles in your honor if you would but let me forget about the maraja."

"You've already forgotten about her." Raimond glanced down at Elionor, and she stared back with her big brown eyes. "I will take her away. I'll give her food, mended clothing, a warm bed." He touched Elionor's head. "And clean hair."

Elionor gripped Raimond's arm tightly with both hands, then threw her arms around him and stayed there. If his own daughter had lived past infancy, she would be waiting at home, ready to embrace him. Now another girl needed him. He would work through the details later, but he would not leave Elionor to rot with this woman, no matter the cost.

"She's uglier than the night anyway, and she's been nothing but a burden to me." Norma scooted her hands up her hips and smirked. "Except I want a back payment for all she's cost me in the last year. Children are expensive, nò?"

"You've taken every ducat she's earned."

Norma scowled at Elionor. "This Raimond thinks he knows everything." She twisted her lips and sniffled loud enough for the whole village square to hear. "But you tell him, maraja. Tell him he's not taking you anywhere without a full pouch of ducats. And not the copper ones. I want silver so shiny I can see my big nose in the reflection."

Raimond shook his head. "I have nothing."

"What's that under your coat?" She eyed the little box near his heart, not hiding her crooked grin. "Any gold in there?"

Raimond pulled his hand up to guard the box. "It's not for you."

"And you somehow expect to feed the girl? And give her a warm bed? Are you stupider than a loaf, or are you just a knife that doesn't cut? The tattered coat, dirt caked on your face, a beard scragglier than an old goat's. You look as if you've crawled up from a cave. Go back to your grotto, you ghost of Saint Joseph! Go back, I say!"

Norma held her copious abdomen with one hand and shooed him away with the other as she roared with laughter.

Of all the women in this realm, why was Norma the one he had to barter with? Raimond glanced to the left, where three men had gathered around a makeshift table outside the tavern—the Burning Heretic, as the sign said. Though they weren't looking now, they'd surely seen something curious outside Norma's abode. Raimond had traveled through too many villages and met too many people to be naive about the position Norma held here. Everyone knew her, and she knew everyone else. And if Raimond didn't stop this cauldron of a woman from boiling over, the entire village would soon know his name. He rubbed the back of his neck with his left hand while Elionor held on to the right.

"Madama . . ." Raimond waited for Norma to finish her name.

"Bifano was my husband's surname. He's dead, and may his bones forever float atop my cesspit."

Then I suppose I shouldn't use that name. "Norma, you might think I'm a vagrant."

"You are."

"*Për piasì*, listen for a moment."

Norma stepped to the side and peered over Raimond's shoulder. "Any good ale in that sack? You look like a man who knows where to find the ale that'll make your eyes fall out, not the watery dross the Burning Heretic sells."

"If you could refrain from interrupting me, I have a way to provide for your payment. First, what's your price?"

Norma scratched her chin. "You don't have a coin to make a maybug dance. Didn't your mima ever tell you, 'A liar is caught quicker than a cripple'?"

"Tell me the price, and I'll pay you."

"Fifty gold florins!" Norma slapped Raimond on the shoulder and snickered.

Raimond brushed off whatever Norma had left on his shoulder. "I need a real price, enough to compensate you for the sacrifices you've made for Elionor." He winced inwardly at his patronizing words, but it should crack Norma's shell.

She ran her tongue under her top lip and made a smacking sound with her mouth. "Ten silver grossi."

Raimond widened his eyes, then looked down at Elionor. Could he truly adopt her? If Maria were here to help, the choice would be simple. For now, he could at least free her from this miserable place. "You'll need to wait a week, maybe less."

"No grossi? No maraja." Norma stood straighter than ever, with her hands around her midsection.

"She needs to eat now, not in a week."

"Then I suppose you should leave now. Or find her some bread. I'll be here, but I won't be waiting. Until then, the maraja will clean the Burning Heretic."

"Let Elionor come with me today. I'll pay you twelve—nò, fifteen—grossi if you release her now."

Norma scowled. "I don't know you, so I can't trust you. No one here in Chivasso knows you." She raised her voice and yelled loud enough for the whole village square to hear. "Does anyone here know this man? Is he honest or a cheat?"

Raimond waited for a snide reply from a bystander, but nothing developed save a few curious stares. Norma had attracted too much attention, and if he didn't close the deal soon, it would end badly for him. "You're right, no one here knows me."

Norma stepped into her house and prepared to shut the door.

Raimond took a step forward. The churches in the mountains would certainly give enough to satisfy Norma. He only needed time. "I can offer far more than you're imagining."

"Where is this fortune you speak of? How much?"

"At least the equivalent of five gold florins."

Norma's eyes brightened. "Five florins?"

"Let me take Elionor now and return as soon as I have your payment."

"Where will you find this gold? If you're the bandit I think you are, don't rob my friends for it—only my enemies."

Raimond gave her a sly grin. Her suspicions might prove to be the key that unlocked her trust. For a moment, he felt as if he were a mischievous boy again. "I'll return by next week."

"Five real gold florins. I have a blacksmith who can verify it too." She narrowed her eyes. "And don't think I won't hunt you down if you don't return with the coins. I know men and women in every village between Chambéry and Venice."

Elionor's hair brushed against Raimond's coat. She looked up and smiled—not a smile of joy or excitement but of contentment. Standing there beside Raimond, she must feel safe. Perhaps for the first time in her life, someone stood for her. And for the first time in years, someone truly needed him.

"If I don't return," Raimond said, "hunt me down and mount my head on your wall."

Norma huffed. "Take the whole week if you wish, but I'd never hang your ugly head over my hearth. I'd rather make soup out of it."

A sound of scuffing feet grew closer from behind. A man's shoulder bumped Raimond before he could turn. "New friend, Norma?"

"This goat just bought my niece from me."

The man leaned toward Raimond and examined him with one eye closed. "I heard he's one of those Vallense preachers from the mountains."

"Don't be a fool, Marino, he's not a—"

"Monsù Raimond does live in the mountains, but he's not a Ballenzee preacher or whatever you said." Elionor glanced at Raimond and smiled for confirmation.

Raimond held his breath as his heart clenched in his chest. He prayed Norma didn't know what Vallense meant.

"Val . . . lense. And you say they live in the mountains?" Norma shot a baleful glance at Raimond. "I should have figured that out earlier. You could have simply told me, Monsù, but I see it now. I know your kind well. It's been a few winters since a Vallense was brave enough to pass through Chivasso."

Raimond squared his shoulders and brought Elionor back under his arm. Marino stood at Norma's right, his stance so far unthreatening. But it was Norma's eyes that made Raimond's pulse quicken. In only two other instances had he seen eyes like that, and both times had ended poorly. "I'll return soon with your payment."

"You're not taking the maraja now."

"We had a deal," Raimond said from behind clenched teeth.

"And yet my hands are empty. Nò, heretic, not for a villa and a thousand barrels of wine would I let you take her now." She lurched forward and grabbed one of Elionor's arms.

"He's not a heretic, not Monsù Raimond!" Elionor screamed.

Raimond pulled Elionor back, but Marino pushed Raimond on both shoulders. Raimond stumbled backward and fell to the snowy ground. He rose to his feet and dusted himself off.

"The last time a Vallense was in Chivasso, we burned him—five or more years ago by my reckoning. So we wouldn't forget him, we named our tavern after the heretic." Norma crossed herself. "May God burn his soul."

Elionor squirmed and twisted her gangly body as Norma held one hand and Marino the other. "Let the child come with me, Norma."

"And let a wicked Vallense like you raise her? Never. I know what men like you do. You slink from village to village, telling lies about the Church, spreading heresy."

Norma paused in thought. Elionor freed her arm from Norma's grip and almost did the same from Marino's. Norma grabbed Elionor's hair and yanked her to the ground.

Raimond leaped forward with his fists up, but again, Marino met him first. He grabbed Raimond's coat, swung him around, and slammed him against the house. Raimond's head burst into pain. His eyesight faded but didn't quite blacken.

"I never believed the rumors about Vallenses stealing children from good Christian families." Norma sniffled and hacked. "But now I see. You think your ways are holy. You roof-sniffers hold your noses so high above the rest of us, thinking you can raise the maraja better than I can." Norma stooped to Elionor's level. "Vallenses imagine they're better than we are. They walk into a village like ours, bring it to a boil, then leave. Listen to me, maraja, you don't want to go with this heretic. He won't feed you, he won't clothe you, and I know he won't love you."

Raimond scanned the village square, where a small crowd of spectators now gawked. If this village held the reputation Norma said it did, he might soon be locked to something he didn't want to be locked to.

Norma stood and waved the onlookers forward. "This man confessed that he's a Vallense preacher! Come, men, do your duty!"

An alley led to the right, away from the square, but Marino was in that path. He wasn't a burly man, but he didn't look weak either. Over twenty years had passed since Raimond's childhood on the streets of Chambéry, but he could still stand for himself. Perhaps others in his profession would have scoffed at the idea, but he had to survive for Elionor.

Raimond gave Marino a quick smile and nod as he swung a low right hook.

His punch sent Marino to the ground like a felled tree. The path was clear. He shook off the pain from his fist and glanced back.

Norma held a hand over Elionor's mouth and gave Raimond the most hateful glare he had yet experienced. She heaved Elionor inside, pulled herself in, and slammed the door.

Raimond reached for the door and pushed, but it refused to budge. He pushed harder, and still nothing. Footsteps pounded toward him from behind. He spun around. One man he could face, two if he were a decade younger than his thirty-five years, but six men? God would have to save Elionor now, for Raimond surely couldn't.

The path to the alley was still open, and Raimond sprinted toward it. This wasn't the first time an enraged mob had chased him, nor would he allow it to be his last.

Instincts from years of fending for himself returned. As he passed a barrel, he toppled it over. Turning into the alley, he pushed every grain of energy into his legs and arms. Ahead, past two houses, open countryside lay before him, but that was where his pursuers would expect him to run. Even if he could outrun them, all they needed was a horseman if they knew where he had fled.

Raimond took a sharp left out of the alley and ran onto a deserted street. After turning right and passing three or four houses, he veered left into another alley. He stopped to rest and peered back around the corner.

No one was on the street. He looked toward the far end of the alley. After a few buildings, it emptied into rolling, snowy hills and a distant patch of trees. By his estimation, that was southwest—exactly the way to the mountains. Though his lungs still begged him for rest, Raimond again leaped into a run, but it wasn't the sprint it had been before.

Safely in the stand of trees, Raimond gazed back toward Chivasso one last time. Smoke billowed from every chimney, painting the cold sky with blotchy streams of gray. The octagonal guard tower rose above the roofs of houses and barns, but the cathedral's bell tower dominated the village. Chivasso was truly enslaved—fastened by chains of vice and indulgence to the institution that professed to watch over the souls of its parishioners. Vallense preachers must have long ago shaken Chivasso's dust from their feet, just as the Savior had bidden His disciples do when a house or city wouldn't hear their words.

Raimond turned his back to the village and strolled to the other side of the woods, catching his breath and praying for little Elionor. Perhaps God never meant him to experience a family after Maria and Azalaïs died. He was supposed to be a *barbe*—an itinerant preacher who forsook home and familiarity for the wild byways that brought him to people who needed his preaching. Five years he had been a barbe, and soon the other barbes would likely have him take a junior partner under his tutelage. Before the next journey, though, he needed to rest somewhere peaceful for a few months—a safe place with plenty of food and, most importantly, fellow believers.

Raimond crossed a bridge over a river filled with ice and came upon the great road that would lead him to Turin and, beyond that, the Vallense homelands. He turned right and walked toward the descending sun.

Yet no matter how much he thought about the Luserna Valley and its refuge, or the friends he would soon see, or the fast-coming alpine spring, his heart refused to surrender Elionor to Chivasso and its depravities.

4

His breath goeth forth, he returneth to his earth; in that very day his thoughts perish.

—Psalm 146:4

TWO FULL DAYS of walking would bring Raimond home. As the sun sank, he held his gaze on the road ahead, not bothering to glance right or left. Save two travelers who passed going the opposite way, he was alone on the road to Turin.

He dared not look back toward Chivasso. The dust of that village lay behind him now, and only God Himself could transform a place like that.

Since he was alone, he might as well quote a psalm or two aloud. The psalms of David brought Raimond the most comfort, so he began with the Thirteenth Psalm.

"'How long wilt thou forget me, O LORD? for ever? how long wilt thou hide thy face from me? How long shall I take counsel in my soul, having sorrow in my heart daily? how long shall mine enemy be exalted over me?'"

God surely hadn't forgotten Raimond. God had been there six years ago when Maria and Azalaïs died. And though evil certainly seemed to rule the world, the Holy Scriptures still held all truth, despite the Roman Church's persistent efforts to stamp them out.

Raimond continued the psalm. "'Consider and hear me, O LORD my God: lighten mine eyes, lest I sleep the sleep of death; Lest mine enemy say, I have prevailed against him; and those that trouble me rejoice when I am moved.'"

Norma had indeed gained the victory today, and that chilled

Raimond below his skin. Who would be Elionor's advocate now? Would she survive another year in that famished state? Or would she survive the squalor only to inherit a miserable womanhood no different from Norma's?

Raimond walked into a small hamlet as the sky behind the distant peaks turned orange. To the left, three children played outside, throwing snowballs at a man ducking behind the corner of a dilapidated house. A woman holding a wooden bowl stepped out of the house and called out. "Children, your soup is ready, so slay your babbo before it cools."

For the first time since Chivasso, Raimond stopped.

The man stepped out from the corner, cradling an armful of snowballs. He let them loose, targeting each of the children but missing every one.

A girl about five years old stuck out her tongue as soon as his arms were empty. "Missed! No water on the Po today, Babbo?"

Raimond smiled. Even the children here knew those unique Piedmontese expressions.

"I'll find my water!" The father charged at the girl and lifted her from the snow. "Angelica, mi cita!" He hoisted her onto his shoulders and waved for the other children to follow. "Your mima is ready. Give yourself a straightening, find a bowl, and tell your mima *mersì*."

Raimond soon stood alone, watching the breath escape from his mouth. The lone sounds were the distant barking of a dog and the whispering flow of the River Po. He reached into his coat pocket, removed the wooden box, and stared at its tiny brass latch. Nearly five years had passed since he had last opened it—far too long. He closed his eyes, took a slow breath, and flipped open the latch.

Two delicate white flowers smiled up at him, and from each— one for Maria and one for Azalaïs—feathery petals radiated outward like spring sunlight after a long alpine winter. Raimond couldn't resist the urge to smile back at them.

Why had he not opened the box earlier? Perhaps he had feared the flowers had become shriveled and deathly, even though a friend had coated them in wax after picking them. But no, they appeared as alive as ever, just as Maria and Azalaïs now were in God's eternal realm.

Raimond lingered over the flowers for a few moments, then closed the latch and placed the box back in the pocket near his heart. The chill of the evening had vanished, replaced with a warm desire to intervene for the sake of a little girl who still breathed in this mortal realm.

What could he do? Surely he couldn't march back into Chivasso, knock on Norma's door, and ask again.

Raimond lifted a hand to his face, but all he touched was a bushy beard—the beard of a defeated wanderer. When was the last time he had trimmed it? He looked down at his clothes, and they were no better. He wore a coat so patched and threadbare that the next gust of wind might shred it into a spray of fragments. His shoes were tattered, his breeches faded from deep brown to a gloomy shade of yellow. It was no wonder everyone had thought he was a vagabond.

He removed the sack from his shoulder and opened it. He never carried much, but everything had a purpose, including the tools every traveler carried: a needle and thread, a knife and sharpening stone, a fire striker and flint, a rough piece of linen for cleaning his teeth. Under the tools was an extra set of clothes. The sack's contents would mean nothing to most, but to Raimond they were the keys to his redemption.

He breathed in the crisp air, then walked toward the sound of the river.

* * *

The light of the setting sun cast a reassuring glow on the otherwise raging River Po. The swift torrent tumbled from right to left, carrying thin sheets of ice and melted snow from all the little mountain streams that flowed into it.

Raimond walked down to the riverbank, set his pack on the ground, and knelt to one knee. His arm tensed the moment his hand touched the icy water, but he resisted the urge to remove it. Though he wouldn't plunge in his whole body, he could wash himself—wash away the grit and grime, wash his eyes, wash his ears, wash his neck, and better reflect the man God desired him to be.

He pulled the knife and sharpening stone from the sack and rubbed a thumb across the blade. After five swipes on the stone for each side of the knife, he felt the edge again. It was sharp enough to cut through an apple but still too dull for his face. He repeated the process until the blade was to his liking.

He began by trimming back the mop of hair he usually hid under his hat. With that finished, he focused on the beard, cutting it back, feeling it with his hand, and trimming it closer. There was also the matter of his neck. He sharpened the knife again, then made small swipes as close to the skin as possible. He winced two or three times when he nicked his skin, but by the time he finished, he felt like a new man. How had he let himself become a derelict?

Barbes like him learned how to preach the gospel, how to find friendly homes when there were none, how to start a fire with nothing but dry sticks, and how best to present themselves to any man, from a lord down to a peasant. But in his five years of being a barbe, no one had taught him to ignore his outward appearance.

Raimond scooped up a handful of his beard from the snow and flipped it into the river. It was no wonder Norma had scoffed at his condition and the villagers had looked at him so oddly. For some reason, Elionor hadn't recoiled, perhaps because of ignorance, or maybe because God had blinded her eyes to Raimond's external form.

Though he had no lye to wash with, Raimond removed his coat and shirt, then splashed water, scrubbed with his hands, and splashed more. The wind had calmed, but he shivered all over. Yet it was a cleansing freeze, the type of cold that peeled off layers of dirt that had collected for weeks. He washed his feet more than once and gave his face a final scrub.

Raimond opened the sack again and grabbed the extra set of clothes. Though far from new, they were like royal garments compared to what he had been wearing. Raimond put on the breeches and shirt, then finished with a fresh pair of wool socks, each of which he fastened with a leather strap below the knee.

His tattered hat and old clothes lay in the snow near the water, but they weren't worth saving. Raimond picked up the rags and, one by one, tossed them into the torrent and watched them flow downstream.

He could not allow the loss of his family to defeat him. Publicly preaching the Holy Scriptures while privately wallowing in his grief did not proclaim a victorious Savior. It wasn't the fault of dear Maria and baby Azalaïs that Raimond grasped for their presence as if they belonged to him but so often neglected the truth of their immortality. He would miss them until the day his body lay buried in the earth, but their memory couldn't be an excuse for his own shortcomings.

Chivasso was the village he had wished never to return to, but now it was his destination. Norma would not defeat him, nor would any of the ruffians from the square. No matter the risk, no matter the price, Raimond would rescue that little outcast of Chivasso, show her the Savior, provide for her, and if God allowed it, be a father to her.

"But I have trusted in thy mercy; my heart shall rejoice in thy salvation." Picking up his sack, he finished the psalm. "I will sing unto the Lord, because he hath dealt bountifully with me."

He slung the sack over his shoulder, turned, and began the trek back to Chivasso. And Elionor.

5

Happy is he that hath the God of Jacob for his help, whose hope is in the LORD his God.

—Psalm 146:5

DOORS CREAKED ON their hinges, dogs barked at the rising full moon, and axes slammed into firewood. Though the night was cool, Chivasso seemed to simmer as Raimond crept through empty alleys, peeked around corners, and ducked under fences.

He passed the Burning Heretic, where the raucous laughter of a Piedmontese tavern flowed out into the night air. After a quick glance around the square, he crept through the shadows to Norma's house. He avoided breathing through his nose and stepped over slop and other manner of stinking things to listen at each window.

"Saint Joseph ran out of Chivasso like a little lizard. He won't be back."

The familiar voice and a slamming door made Raimond hurry off to a nearby alcove hidden from the evening twilight. He turned to listen, hoping to discover Elionor's whereabouts.

"You said that years ago when we burned that heretic," said another voice, "and still those Vallenses returned."

"One Vallense." Norma stepped from the shadows only a few paces away. "And he was as young as garlic. I say he's never heard what we do to their kind here, or any who so much as give them old crumbs."

"At least the secret is safe," the man said in a hushed voice.

"Not while your master still breathes." Norma coughed loud

enough to wake the whole village. "I'll have no rest until he's covered in dirt."

"What should I do with the girl? It's becoming too risky having her so near."

"She's a child," Norma said. "A dirty, frightened wretch who cares for nothing but that terror of a cat."

"Where is she now?"

"I almost wish I would've let that heretic take her. Maybe then everyone would stop asking me that ridiculous question. She's not mine. I hate everything she says, I hated her foolish mother, and I hate her. Last I knew, she ran from my house in tears, probably off to spend the night under someone's eaves again." Norma spat on the ground and rubbed the spittle into the snow with her foot.

Raimond stepped back but brushed against a stack of crates. A cat bounded out, toppling the crates and whatever was in them. Something sharp slammed into Raimond's elbow. He winced and held in a grunt.

"What was that?" the man asked.

Norma put a finger to her lips.

Now was not the time to confront Norma or this mysterious man. Raimond scanned for a clear path of escape and settled on the same one the cat had chosen. Though his elbow still throbbed, he pushed away from the alcove and bounded into the street.

"It's a man!" Norma shouted. "Hail! Who's there?"

Raimond didn't stop to answer. He pressed forward through the dark streets until he burst onto the road leading south toward the river. Before long he found the barn where he'd spent the last night, and after a quick glance to be sure no one was following, he pulled the door open and stepped inside.

The sound of his own thumping heartbeat met him. Something crashed into his legs. Raimond clenched his fists, ready for a fight.

Another strike, this time on only one leg. Whatever was hitting him wasn't using all its strength, unless—

"Elionor?"

"Monsù Raimond?"

Two bony arms wrapped around him. Elionor's matted hair

brushed Raimond's arm as he held her close. He could joyfully endure more hugs like this.

"You came back! Magna said you were afraid and ran away and you'd never return." Elionor rubbed her eyes and sobbed.

Raimond bent down, wrapped an arm around her, and let her weep into his coat. "I am back, I won't leave you again, and I won't let Norma hurt you."

Elionor's crying continued, but after a few moments, she lifted her head, wiped the tears from her cheeks, and gave Raimond a curious look. "You look different."

"A much-needed change of clothes, a trim, and a shave—something I should have done days ago. And let me show you something." Raimond removed the wooden box from his pocket and opened it toward Elionor.

"Those are pretty flowers." She tilted her head and grinned. "What are they for?"

"It was springtime in the mountains when my wife and baby died, and a dear friend named Magdalena Janavel picked these two flowers for me and coated them in wax so they would last. I've kept them in this box so I would never forget my family, and now you're one of the few to see them." Raimond placed the box in Elionor's hand.

"They look like daisies," she said as she examined them, "but there are so many long petals."

"Flowers like this bloom high in the mountains every spring, but only for a short time. Around here, people call them *stèila alpin*, and that means—"

"Alpine star! They do look like little stars."

"Sì, and the Germans who live far in the north have a different word for them: *edelweiss*, which means 'noble and white.' Then there are my people, and to us, the name is *immortèla*. Elionor, these flowers are incredibly special. We call them immortèlas because they remind us of something divine. There is a place called heaven, a beautiful realm where those who believe the gospel of Jesus Christ go to be with God and live in joy forever." Raimond pointed at the pure white flowers. "These represent that eternal life in heaven, and they remind me that though my wife and baby are no longer with me, I will see them again. When I look at these immortèlas, I remember my love for my family and the promise of eternal life the Holy Scriptures teach us."

Elionor gently closed the box and gave it back to Raimond. "I wish I could have known your wife and baby. What were their names?"

"Maria was my wife, and Azalaïs my daughter. Maria would have adored you, for her heart was always set on others." Raimond swallowed as he dropped the box into his pocket. "Something I have tried to carry on myself."

"What was that word Magna called you?"

Raimond shrugged. "A heretic? Saint Joseph?"

"Nò, I think she said *Ballenzee*."

"Ah sì, Vallense—that's one of the names of my people. Others have named us Waldensians or Vaudois. We are mainly farmers and shepherds, but what makes us different is our obedience to the Holy Scriptures instead of the Church's traditions."

"Are you a farmer?"

"For a short time I was, but now I'm a barbe."

"Uncle!" Elionor laughed. "Why are you called an uncle?"

"That's a question I can't answer, though I've heard some say it's meant to be different from the priests. What do the people here call their priest?"

"*Padre*, I think."

"The Holy Scriptures say, 'And call no man your father upon the earth: for one is your Father, which is in heaven.' So instead of *padre*, Vallenses call men like me barbes. We travel to many lands to encourage other Vallenses and preach the gospel to all who will listen."

"I want to be a Vallense." Elionor smiled and placed her hand in Raimond's. "Do you know any little girls like me?"

"I do! There are Catherine Lauras and Inès de Pratis, and my good friend Nicolaus Pavarin's youngest is about your age. Her name is Constanza."

"I'm ready to leave now. Rosmarin too. May she come to the mountains with us?"

"Rosmarin may come, but we can't leave yet." Raimond touched

Elionor's cheek. How would she understand? "Before we leave, we must first gain your magna's permission."

"Her what?"

"You can't leave until Norma approves."

Elionor's chin shook, and her eyes emptied of life. "She'll never let me go."

"Nò, and I can't make her, not by myself."

"Për piasì, Monsù Raimond, don't go to Magna. We should leave now, because if we don't, she'll try to hurt you again."

"I don't want to be hurt, but sometimes God wants us to risk our own safety so we can help others."

"Anyone but Magna. I know she'll do whatever bad things she says."

Raimond stood but kept his hand on Elionor's shoulder. "Your magna was in the square this evening, talking—"

"She always talks."

"I've discovered that, but she referred to someone's master with a particular hatred."

"She hates everybody." Elionor remained straight-faced.

"Whom does she hate more than everyone else? Or is there someone she fears?"

"Rosmarin, but she's a cat, not a man." Elionor widened her eyes. "Maybe Monsù Damiano."

"Remind me who that is."

"Remember what I told you? This is his barn."

"Ah sì, I remember. He's the man who pays you three ducats per month. Why would your magna hate him?"

"I think she's afraid of Monsù Damiano. She's the one who told me all the stories about him before I worked here. Then she made me swear to never go near his door, or else he'll chop me up and make me into pig slop. Or he'll eat me himself."

Raimond nodded and half smiled. "Perhaps we should meet this Monsù Damiano."

Elionor shook her head. "Nò. Për piasì."

"Somehow Norma sees this Damiano as her enemy. That may help us."

"I can't." Elionor's tears fell again as she clamped on to his legs.

Raimond patted her shoulder. "I've met many wicked people in this world. Those men are hurting inside more than you or I can see. Sin rots all men and women from the inside out. Those who are mean and angry have let all that rot come out, and now everyone sees it. Yet I have also seen seemingly kind and joyful people commit the same sins. They are only better at hiding the sin in their hearts."

"I don't sin," Elionor said in all seriousness.

Raimond pulled his head back. "Never?"

"Three or four times, but they were little sins."

"You have much to learn, dear Elionor, but all in time. First, I will bring you to a place where you're free to learn about God and all matters of the heart. We can talk all night, but that won't change Norma's mind." Raimond stooped down to Elionor's level and held her shoulders. "We need to talk to Damiano. He may be our one hope of solving this problem with Norma."

"You can go."

"I need you to be brave—braver than you've ever been. If I go to Monsù Damiano's door by myself, he'll dismiss me. When men speak to other men, they speak about everything as if it were a trade. I don't want that. But when a woman or a child is there—"

"What can I do?"

"You wouldn't need to do anything except be there. You don't have to dance or juggle or sing."

"I can't do any of those things."

"Someday I'll teach you to sing and pray, but all you must do tonight is stand by my side and smile, even when you're afraid. The smile of a child sweetens hearts, especially the bitterest ones."

Elionor patted her leg, and soon Rosmarin was in her arms. "Can she come too?"

Raimond scratched the cat behind its ears. "I suppose."

As soon as Raimond and Elionor stepped from the barn, Rosmarin leaped from Elionor's arms. Raimond grabbed Elionor's hand to keep her from chasing the cat.

"We need to find her!"

"After we speak to Monsù Damiano."

"She's scared, and she's . . . I'm . . ."

As Elionor whimpered, something rustled in a nearby hedgerow. Then came a mischievous cackle.

Raimond stepped in front of Elionor. "Stay behind me."

From the hedges stumbled five boys—by their height, each about ten years old. Raimond sighed in relief. One boy carried an empty wine sack, and the others swayed as they walked. They must have been drinking.

The tallest boy turned toward Raimond and Elionor and took a few unsteady steps. "Look, it's the wretch Elionor Casto and her new *demòni*."

Before sunset, Raimond had been Saint Joseph, and now this boy was calling him a demon. But the way he slurred his words. He was too young to be so drunk. A childhood like this would lead to only misery later in life, the same misery from which Raimond was trying to save Elionor.

"That's Santino," Elionor whispered to Raimond. "He and the other boys always try to make me cry." She stepped forward and crossed her arms. "His name is Monsù Raimond, and he's not a demòni."

A rock flew at them, barely missing Elionor's head. Raimond stepped in front of her again. "Boys, it's late. Go back to your babbos and mimas."

"They're drunk too." Santino held up the wine sack. "How else could we steal this?"

A few of the boys moved to the sides, trying to surround Raimond and Elionor. They were seeing how strong Raimond was and, more importantly, if he had anything they wanted. Twenty years or more ago, Raimond had often used the same tactic: pummel a stranger, rob him, and spend the coins on ale and, if he was hungry, a loaf of bread. But God had forgiven him for that. As a newly married man, he had met an old barbe in the Chambéry market and listened to the words from the Holy Scriptures—those same wonderful words God had now given him to preach.

He threw his sack on the ground and showed the boys his hands. "I don't have anything you want."

"Give me your book of spells, demòni."

"Spell book? I'm no sorcerer."

"You all have one," another boy said from behind Santino. "My babbo said all demònis carry a book."

Raimond threw his head back and laughed. "A Bible? You want a Bible. Regretfully, I don't have one now, but I can return someday and show you—"

"I don't want your spells," Santino said between hiccups. "I want your coins. Give them to us, or we'll leave you here in the cold with no clothes."

"Nò you won't, you dog!" Elionor shouted. "Monsù Raimond is from the mountains, and he's stronger than all of you."

Santino waved the other boys forward. "Let's find out."

Raimond patted Elionor on the shoulder. "Go to the barn and shut the door. We'll leave soon." He turned to the boys, stretching his arms and flexing his fingers. "You don't want to do this, boys. It's not worth it."

"We'll find out by the end of this," Santino said.

All at once the boys ran at Raimond. Two went for his legs, while another came at his midsection. Raimond tripped one boy and stepped on his back, but not hard. Their drinking had made them weak and unbalanced. By the time he threw another two boys to the ground, the last two held their distance.

Raimond shook his head and glanced at the three on the ground. "I've been in more fights than you can count, but I don't want to fight you. If you insist on brawling with me, though, you'll all be eating snow."

The three on the ground teetered as they tried to stand, and a tinge of guilt struck Raimond. If it weren't for defending Elionor, he would have let them relish their fun. But this wasn't a fair fight. It didn't matter that there were five boys; they were still boys, and drunk ones too. "Stop this before you end up with a bloody nose or a bruised knee."

Santino stood straight, fists clenched but shaking. "I'll tell my padre you tried to rob us."

"Do it, but soon Elionor and I will be far away."

"I'll . . . I'll tell Norma you took Elionor. Then our padres will hunt you down like the last heretic."

A rock landed far in front of the boys and rolled toward them, completely missing its mark.

Elionor stepped beside Raimond and crossed her arms. "See, I told you he was strong! Leave us be!"

Raimond shushed her. "Don't give them a reason to be angry, cita. 'A soft answer turneth away wrath: but grievous words stir up anger.'"

"But they—"

"You're no better than they are if you poke and prod. Let them flee."

Four of the boys ran off immediately. Santino grabbed his wine sack first. "Throw yourself in the Po, Elionor Casto. Your stench sickens me." He stared Elionor down, then turned and hobbled away.

Elionor threw herself into Raimond's arms, weeping.

"Don't fret about what they said. We'll soon be far from here, and we'll find you warm water, lye, and perhaps some dried flower petals."

"I tried to pick the bugs from my hair, but they always come back. I asked Magna, and she pushed me away. Can you help?"

"I lack the experience for proper louse removal, but I know friends who will help. If you'd like to be rid of those pests first, then that's what it will be."

"Do we still have to see Monsù Damiano? Remember, he has red eyes, green hair, sharp fingernails—"

"If you only heard what people say about me." Raimond set Elionor back on her feet just as Rosmarin scampered out from the shadows.

"I know. They called you a demòni."

"Which is tame compared to other names. But that doesn't matter. God keeps me safe, and He'll protect me until my work on earth is finished."

"When will it be finished?"

"That I don't know. It might be today, or it might be when I'm old. Ignorance of the future is a gift from God, not a curse, for I must always be prepared—serving, praying, preaching, and giving."

"We can go see Monsù Damiano now." Elionor picked up Rosmarin and stood alongside Raimond. "Can I stay behind you?"

"*Già che*. Certainly, and if his eyes are truly green—"

"Nò, red eyes."

Raimond laughed inwardly and led Elionor up the hill to Damiano's villa.

6

Which made heaven, and earth, the sea, and all that therein is: which keepeth truth for ever.

—Psalm 146:6

Vines and moss clung to the sides of what might have once been an attractive villa. Raimond pushed aside the spray of ivy that hung over the top half of the door as Elionor stood beside him, cradling Rosmarin.

"I'm praying we don't wake anyone," Raimond said under his breath.

"Monsù Damiano doesn't sleep. At night, he boils the feet of puppies and eats them."

"Along with the eggs you gather for him every day?"

Elionor gave a few abrupt nods.

"I've met many unusual people—fire-eaters, a one-legged wrestler, a man dressed in rags who claimed to be the pope. But I've never met a green-haired, red-eyed puppy-eater."

His shallow knock felt as if it would burst through the rotted, mildewed wood. He and Elionor waited, but nothing acknowledged them, not even the echo of an empty house.

Raimond glanced over his shoulder at Elionor. "Are you sure someone lives here?"

She fastened her lips shut but nodded twice.

Fearing he would shatter the door if he knocked in the same place, Raimond aimed closer to the hinges and knocked harder. Again, nothing.

Then there was a thud. And footsteps. Elionor held Rosmarin

tight under her chin and hid her eyes. The footsteps drew closer and finally stopped.

A muffled voice spoke through the door. "Hail! Who calls at this late hour?"

That voice. I've heard it before.

"Raimond Durand of Valle dë Luserna. I request an audience with Monsù Damiano."

The door flung open, and there stood a man whose nose was nearly above Raimond's brow. The man's long face bore no expression, and his shoulders slumped forward. Behind him, flickering candles cast a yellow glow on empty stucco walls.

"Are you Damiano?" Raimond asked.

Elionor tugged on his coat and whispered, "Nò, that's Ago, the servant."

Ago glared at Elionor and took a step backward. "You were told to never approach this door! Never!" He took a deep breath as his hands shook. Why was he so angry?

"Mi scusa, I didn't want to come, but Monsù Raimond—"

"Norma will hear of this by tomorrow!" Ago looked at Raimond, deepened his scowl, and raised an arm across his chest, ready to backhand Raimond.

A powerful voice bellowed from deep in the house. "Who's at my door?"

Ago turned and answered, this time in a gentle tone. "Only beggars like the last time."

"I heard the voice of a child."

"As I said, *Maestro*, beggars trying to take what little food we have."

A light tapping echoed from inside. Ago scratched his shoulder. "Maestro—"

"Would you spurn a hungry child on my doorstep?" Footsteps were now interspersed with the taps.

"We aren't here to beg." Raimond stood on his toes, trying to see behind Ago. "I need only a moment of Monsù Damiano's evening."

A man with a cane stepped in front of Ago. A white cloth was wrapped around his head, covering his eyes. Two deep scars ran across his left cheek, and dark, thick hair with a few specks of gray drooped over his ears and brow. He couldn't have been much older than Raimond, though—perhaps forty. "I am Damiano Rivera," he said in a clear, deep voice.

Elionor let Rosmarin down and grabbed Raimond's hand as he bowed low.

"One name I heard—Raimond—but who is this girl I hear?" Damiano revealed a little smile. "Do you know how many months have passed since the voice of a child entered my ears?"

Ago tugged on Damiano's sleeve. "Maestro, the hour is late, and these people are here to take advantage of you."

Damiano waved him off. "Stop speaking. I hear enough of your voice. The girl. I want to hear that voice again."

Raimond nudged Elionor. "Tell him your name."

"Për piasì, what is your name?" Damiano tapped his cane on the ground and took a step down from the door.

Elionor clung tighter to Raimond. Her body shook.

"She's scared," Raimond said. "There are rumors in the village—"

"This man chatters but brings no facts." Ago squinted at Raimond but spoke to Damiano. "All in Chivasso greatly respect the name of Damiano Rivera. No one fears you, Maestro. Now let us be rid of these vagrants."

Damiano swung his cane wide and struck Ago's legs. "Prepare my table for two guests."

Ago rubbed his legs and sniffed. "Perhaps instead—"

Again Damiano hit him with the cane, this time on the shins. "Me, two guests, and no more objections from you."

Ago sneered at Raimond and Elionor, spun around, and marched inside.

"My servant can be shy." Damiano motioned for Elionor and Raimond to follow him inside. "Come, eat at my table and tell me your plight."

"You are generous." Raimond bowed again and took a step toward the door, but Elionor kept her feet planted.

"He's hiding his eyes behind that cloth," she said. "When we're inside, he'll—"

"Do you see the kindness he shows us?"

"But it's so dark in there."

"The candles will light our way. Never doubt a well-lit path, even when shadows lie around you."

"Rosmarin?"

"She can wait for us." Raimond again pulled gently. This time Elionor followed.

Damiano used his cane to feel his way through the hall, then turned left into a room with a hearth. Raimond followed close behind with Elionor's trembling hand locked to his. At the hearth, Ago stirred a bubbling pot of what looked like a vegetable stew.

Damiano tapped his cane against a wooden table and swept his hand across its surface. "Ago, this side of the table is filthy."

Ago winced and dropped the spoon into the kettle. "We never use that side of the table, so whom would I help by wiping it?"

"I give you a warm home, I feed you, and you reward me by wearing out all the chairs in my house." Damiano tapped the tabletop with his cane. "Come, wipe this table."

"Sì, maestro."

Raimond waved Ago back. "Where are the rags? I'll wipe it."

"Who are you, Raimond Durand of Valle dë Luserna?" Damiano asked.

Raimond pressed his lips together and swallowed. "I am but a lone traveler returning from a journey far to the north, beyond the Alps."

"You have come a long way, traveler, but what brings you to Chivasso and onto the doorstep of my home?"

"I stopped here to rest last night. In the morning, I met Elionor in your barn."

"Elionor?" Damiano gasped and brought a hand to his heart. "Elionor? Is this the daughter of Vilfred Casto?"

Elionor loosened her grip on Raimond's hand but didn't answer.

"Nò," Ago said. "As I told you, Vilfred's daughter has been bedridden since last winter, before you returned from the crusade."

Damiano ignored Ago and shuffled toward Elionor, tapping

his cane in a left-right-forward pattern. "Your age, cita—what is your age?"

Elionor glanced up at Raimond, then at Damiano.

"You're safe," Raimond said, releasing her hand and giving her a reassuring pat on the shoulder.

"Seven." Elionor cast her timid gaze to the side.

"Precisely as I had guessed. Ago! Ago!" There was no answer. "This is truly Elionor Casto. How did . . . why . . ." He trailed off.

Ago drifted from the hearth toward Damiano, giving Raimond a piercing glare on the way. "Vespers have passed, and your mind is weary." He grasped Damiano's arm and pointed him toward the door. "I'll rewarm the stew in the morning after you rest."

Raimond stepped forward and shot a sidelong glance at Ago. "Monsù Damiano is capable of making his own decisions."

"My own decisions, sì. I am no old man." Damiano brushed away Ago's hand. "Tell me now, is this Elionor, daughter of Vilfred Casto?"

"My babbo's name was Vilfred." Elionor's voice was soft and shaky. "I think."

Damiano struck Ago with his cane, then fell to his knees. "Oh, dear child." He made the sign of the cross. "By the grace of Saint Raphael the Archangel, you are healed!"

Elionor looked up for guidance, and Raimond nodded toward Damiano. After a moment of hesitation, Elionor took a step.

"Come to me, cita, për piasì, come. You have nothing to fear in this house." Damiano reached out but grasped only air. His voice shook. "Where are you?"

Elionor bit her lip and took two more steps. As Damiano embraced her, she stood straight with her hands at her sides. "I'm not sick, Monsù. I haven't been. And I don't have a bed, except for the mat in the barn."

Damiano frowned. Ago reached a hand out to him. "Maestro—"

"The child says she hasn't been sick. Why would you lie about such a thing? Why would Norma lie?" Damiano nestled Elionor's head down on his shoulder. "Are you hungry? Oh, you are nothing but bones, cita. I may not serve you the tongues of canaries, but what I have will fill your belly."

Elionor gulped and stood as stiff as a road sign. "Tongues of canaries?"

"Ah, that means I have nothing fancy to eat here." He hugged her tighter. "But where have you been this last year, cita?"

By the dull look in her eyes, she was as confused as Raimond was. He answered for her. "Norma is somewhat of a guardian to her, but that would give the woman too much praise."

"That evil *patelavache* hasn't fed you! She told me you were on the verge of death. I have been sending money for your care for over a year." Damiano took a long breath. "It's my fault. I should have visited you, but I was afraid my disfigurement would terrify you." He grabbed his cane and stood. "I shouldn't have believed the words of my servant . . . whom I have always compensated generously." He turned toward Ago. "Where is the money I have been sending Norma for Elionor's healing? Where is it?"

"Understand, Maestro, my mother is a widow, and now I'm her only child. She has no way to support herself, and Norma offered me a chance—"

"Leave this house and never return."

"Who will cook for you? Who will sweep the floors and wash your clothes?"

"Not you! Never! You are a scheming thief. Crawl back to Norma and tell her I know everything, and soon everyone else shall know."

Ago huffed, gave Raimond a sly glance, and skittered from the room.

"I don't know where to begin," Damiano said. "Everything around me is collapsing. I trusted Ago, but I shall forever regret that choice. Forever."

The smells from the hearth streamed toward Raimond, drawing his gaze to the kettle. The stew was boiling over. He sprang toward the hearth, grabbed a cloth, and lifted the lid.

"I suppose it's ready now," Damiano said, "and since Ago won't be dining with us, there will be plenty for all."

Raimond's mouth watered, and his body begged for the slightest of tastes. He lifted a spoonful from the kettle, cooled it with a few puffs, and dropped some onto his tongue. His stomach yearned for more, but Elionor needed it far more than he did. "Taste this, Elionor."

"Bring the kettle to the table so we may enjoy it together." Damiano reached for Elionor again. "I have many questions, and I imagine you do as well."

As soon as Raimond ladled the stew into Elionor's bowl, she lifted it to her mouth and slurped loudly.

"When was the last time you've eaten, cita?" Damiano waited for Raimond to serve him, then drank, but not as obviously.

Elionor wiped her mouth with her sleeve but didn't set down the bowl. "Monsù Raimond gave me a hunk of bread this morning. And yesterday I ate some old bread the baker gave Ago. It was for the pigs, but I was so hungry and—"

"It is I who should apologize." Damiano shook his head slowly. "I have failed you utterly."

Raimond served himself last, and after a brief prayer of thanksgiving, he sat and faced Damiano. Somewhere past the mystery that enveloped the man across from him—under the scars, beneath the cloth over his eyes—was a soul. "Monsù, we know nothing. I came to you because Elionor is in need. Norma treats her like a stray dog, and her parents are dead."

"I knew her father. His name was Vilfred Casto, and he was like a brother to me. We fought side by side in a land far from here." Damiano tilted his head down, his tone somber. "And a terrible land it was, one to which I will never return."

Raimond glanced down at Elionor, whose bowl was now empty. Sitting up on her knees, she pushed her bowl toward the kettle and stretched for the spoon, but she couldn't reach it.

"Let me serve you." Raimond took the bowl and filled it again.

"Once I could serve others as you do." Damiano rubbed a hand across his scarred cheek. "Young women swooned over me. I was strong, a blacksmith like my father. I could hold a shield and the heaviest halberd. Nothing in the world could slow me." He motioned toward his eyes. "Then this happened, and now I will live out my years in darkness. It's been nearly two years now, two years since . . ."

He trailed off. Elionor's slurping and the fire's crackling were the only sounds in the room.

Damiano leaned closer to Raimond and lowered his voice. "The last images that fell upon these eyes—forever imprinted on the canvas of my mind—are blood, fire, and death. I pray daily that God would open my eyes for a moment, only so I could glimpse a vineyard on rolling hills, or the face of a beautiful woman, or a single white rose in the dawn twilight. Perhaps then the roar of battle and the desperate screams of the dying would not plague my mind."

What could Raimond say? He had met men with battle scars, both seen and unseen, but they needed more than empty, lifeless words. Surely Damiano needed to experience the love of God and His Son, but even then, he would still be blind, and those raw memories would still linger.

Damiano set his bowl on the table and reached toward Elionor. Raimond gave her a nod, encouraging her to help. She touched Damiano's hand, and he responded by grasping it.

"Your father gave his life so I might live. I watched him draw his final breath, but before that, he made me swear I would take care of his only child."

"Where did he die?" Elionor asked.

Damiano's bottom lip trembled. "Vilfred Casto died on the battlefield like a warrior from the legends. It was far to the east, near a place called Niš. The pope called for a crusade against the Turks, and we answered that call. Your father, dear Elionor, was a hero."

"That's not what Magna says. 'Vilfred was a fool for leaving,' she says."

"Norma." Damiano released Elionor's hand and leaned back in his chair. "That viper cheated me, and I'm afraid I'll never know the depth of her deceptions."

Raimond ladled another bowl of stew for himself. "Why does Norma fear you?"

"She fears her brother's last confession. She fears the knowledge he once held and what it means for her and her friends." Damiano sighed. "But that is something I will rectify at another time. We all know now that she feared I would discover her schemes against the child." He rested his hands on the table. "After Vilfred saved my life, I fought for another month, until the Turks turned back our army at Zlatitsa. It was there I was maimed in battle, and it was there my eyes last glimpsed the sunlight. Yet I lived, and I swore to God Himself that I would fulfill my vow to Vilfred Casto."

Elionor took another loud slurp from her bowl. "How did you come here if you can't see?"

"Friends guided me to Chivasso, and then I tried to find you. Unfortunately, I met Norma first."

"I lived in Magna's house when Babbo first left." Elionor's face fell. "She was always cruel, but when she told me Babbo had died, she made me sleep outside and work in the barn—your barn, Monsù."

"Are you the girl who worked for Ago?" Damiano brought his hands to his forehead. "Everything, every betrayal, was directly before me. Yet because of this"—he swung a hand toward the cloth over his eyes—"I have failed Vilfred."

"Why would Norma lie to you about Elionor?" Raimond asked. "What did she gain?"

"Apparently what little money I had. I was never wealthy, but I gained some loot after we captured Niš. I had planned to buy a small villa, continue blacksmithing, and perhaps cultivate a few rows of grapevines. When I was wounded, however, those plans changed to simply finding Chivasso and supporting Vilfred's daughter. Nò, I could never be her father in this condition, but I could provide. When I told Norma about her brother's death, she shed some tears, but when I told her I would provide for Elionor, she stuttered." Damiano shook his head. "She told me Elionor had become terribly ill and required constant care to stay alive. So I have been sending money to Norma every week, and I vowed to remain here in Chivasso until Elionor was healthy again."

Elionor squinted at Damiano. "All the village children say your eyes are red and your hair is green."

"Yet another lie from Ago and Norma, I would guess. Every week when I send the money, I ask Ago about your condition. 'A burning fever,' he says one week, and 'No appetite' the next. Each day I have prayed to Saint Raphael for your healing. Meanwhile Chivasso has offered me solitude—a place to sift through my memories and search for God. Now I rent this once-abandoned villa, and Ago helped me care for it. Or so he said."

Raimond scanned the room. Ashes and dirt were piled around the hearth; cobwebs hung from the ceiling; dirty dishes and rags were scattered on top of another table.

"I haven't left this house in over a year, trusting Ago to take the money to Norma, fetch my provisions, and otherwise steward this small plot of land." Damiano reached for the bandage around his eyes. "Please don't be frightened." He pulled the bandage over the top of his head. A deep gash ran from his right temple across a closed and mutilated eyelid, through the bridge of his nose, and finally to the left eye, which was even more grotesque than the right. "Look at me now—miserable, blind, and a fool who has let two schemers steal my wealth and trample a little girl as if she were mud on their boots."

Elionor pushed her bowl away and examined Damiano. Her expression showed some uncertainty, but not disgust. "You've helped me, Monsù Damiano. Three ducats per month. I sleep in your barn most nights. I found a cat there too. Her name is Rosmarin."

"Rosmarin! A cat with a name!" Damiano nodded and showed a little smile, then wrapped his eyes again. "You are a lily amid a thatch of briars, cita. At least now I can make this right—after I bestow upon Norma her long-overdue punishment."

Elionor rubbed her eyes, stretched, and yawned.

"The child is tired," Damiano said. "Time for you to rest somewhere quiet."

"Rosmarin is probably waiting for me. I'll go to the barn."

"*Mi pòvra cita*, you will not! I have no beds to spare here, but you can sleep by the hearth tonight. The blankets are . . ." Damiano rose and grabbed his cane, then stopped. "I don't know where they might be. I suppose the storeroom, but I'm not sure where that is from here."

Raimond laid a hand on Damiano's shoulder. "I'll find them."

He whispered a prayer as he searched for the blankets. "Thank You for providing me with a way to save Elionor. It was You who led me to Damiano, and it is You alone who sustains me. You have made Your strength perfect in my weakness. And Your grace is sufficient."

After Raimond wrapped Elionor with blankets near the hearth, he sat at the table again. Damiano cleared his throat. "Valle dë Luserna, you say, but your accent tells me otherwise. Tell me, traveler, from where do you truly hail?"

"Across the western mountains in Savoy. There the dialect is like your own, but it has its differences too."

"What made you move from Savoy to Piedmont? And of all places in this realm, why Valle dë Luserna? I am quite familiar with the area because I spent most of my life near there. Pinerolo—I imagine you know the city."

"Sì, I know Pinerolo." Raimond's pulse quickened. If Damiano was from Pinerolo, he would know who lived in the Luserna Valley. Since he had answered the pope's call for a crusade against the Turks, he must be a devout Catholic. And if he guessed Raimond was a Vallense—or, worse, a barbe—he would never allow him to take Elionor home to the valley.

"I've been to Valle dë Luserna many times, especially as a young man selling my father's products in the La Torre market."

"I'm rarely home." Raimond swallowed hard and leaned on one elbow. "My wife and I moved there almost ten years ago, and now she is buried there." He glanced toward the child curled up near the hearth. If life had taken a different path, he might have had a daughter like her. What would life have been like if Maria and Azalaïs had lived? Could this be his opportunity to have someone else to live for, to raise a child in love and faith in God?

"You are uneasy, Raimond Durand. My eyes may not serve me as yours serve you, but I can feel the nervousness in the air. I can hear it in the wisps of your breath." Damiano leaned forward and quieted his voice. "You are in far more danger than you realize. Your secrets are safe in my house, but beyond these walls—"

"I'm not sure what you're referring to, Monsù. I'm not nervous or uneasy. Now, let's speak about Elionor."

"Caution on your part—that's all I'm insisting. I know something about Norma few others would guess, even in Chivasso. Before Vilfred died, he told stories about his life here in Piedmont. An engaging storyteller he was, and he could gather a crowd of soldiers like none other. I can almost smell the campfires now, and I can imagine the glowing embers. One of his favorite stories was about a group he and his sister had joined—l'Órdin dla Santa Cros. Are you familiar with that name?"

"The Order of the Holy Cross," Raimond repeated. "It could be the name of any Church confraternity."

"It is a confraternity, but it's so much more. It has spun its web in villages of every size, from Pinerolo to Asti and from here to Saluzzo. Vilfred often spoke of it. Its purpose is to detect heresy, flush it out, and extinguish it. Informants lean against tavern doors, listening for anything contrary to the Apostles' teaching. Some pretend to follow heretical teachings so they might spy on those spreading such teachings. And this league is growing, perhaps in Chivasso more than elsewhere. Vilfred said he was the leader of the local chapter here, but he left his surveillance responsibilities with Norma before he went on the crusade."

Raimond leaned back and crossed his arms. "This is all interesting information, but you're grinding water in the mortar by telling me. I'm nothing but a traveler who saw a little orphan girl and now wants to adopt her." He paused to gather the right words. "I need your help to gain Norma's consent."

Damiano nodded slowly. "*An efet.* But the more you speak, Raimond Durand, the more you reveal yourself. You don't swear, you're not a brawler, you live in Valle dë Luserna, you have shown compassion to Elionor. Perhaps you'll preach to me next, but I think you'll still deny who you are."

Raimond closed his eyes and almost blurted out the truth, but now wasn't the right moment. Night had settled on Chivasso, and time was dwindling. If this Order of the Holy Cross had spread its net in Chivasso, then Raimond must leave with Elionor soon. "Can you help us?"

"I vowed to Vilfred that I would support his daughter. I have failed, but I know you won't. Having spoken much to Vilfred, I feel he might approve of Elionor being raised by . . ." Damiano bit his lip.

"Why would her crusading father approve of her being raised by . . . people like me?"

"That is a story I cannot tell. Not yet. Not until I confront that liar, Norma Bifano."

"You will go to her then? When?"

"I have not left this house in over a year, but I won't let this opportunity fly over my head. Tomorrow at first light—you must tell me when that is—you can lead me to Norma, and I promise you, she will relinquish her claims of guardianship. If she refuses, I'll tell the magistrate all about her thievery. He may be on her side now, even though I have papers to prove my guardianship, but he won't be when he hears what I know."

Elionor stirred near the hearth and pulled the blanket to her chin. When was the last time she had slept in comfort?

A click and a loud crash echoed from the hallway. Raimond glanced at Elionor, but she remained asleep.

"The door." Damiano stood and turned his ear to the hall. "Who could that be at this hour?"

Footsteps.

"Ago, I hear your diddling steps! I told you to never return!"

There were more steps now, rushing closer. Raimond ran to Elionor.

But as soon as Raimond held the half-asleep girl in his arms, Ago stepped into the room. Three men with torches appeared behind him. Last came a man wearing dark robes and a gold cross, panting, coughing, and wiping his brow.

"Come with us, heretic." The priest glared at him and pointed at Elionor. "She's a Catholic girl, and she isn't going anywhere."

Damiano stretched out his hands, palms facing upward. "What is this madness, Ago? I forbade you from stepping into the house again, and here you are, not more than an hour later, and with a priest no less."

Raimond scanned the room for a clear exit. Ago and another man blocked the door, and two others flanked it on either side.

There was no other opening, not even a window. He held Elionor close. Her limbs shook. "Don't fear," Raimond whispered. "God is with us, and He won't fail us."

Elionor peeked over Raimond's shoulder. "I don't see Him."

"You can't escape the judgment of God." The priest scowled at Raimond. "We're all here, and we all know who you are."

Raimond ignored him and whispered to Elionor, "Hold tight."

As soon as Elionor nodded, he burst into a run.

Raimond turned the shoulder opposite Elionor and rammed into Ago. The man hit the wall, but another grabbed for Elionor. Raimond pulled away, but in an instant, two more men surrounded him.

They ripped Elionor away. Raimond reached for her. Someone swept his feet out from under him. His knees slammed onto the stone floor.

Elionor screamed and kicked at her captors. "Nò, nò! Stop!"

The priest kicked Raimond to the ground and put a foot on his chest. "We've already called for the chief inquisitor in Turin. He'll be here in a few days."

Raimond lurched up. Then came a kick to his jaw. He winced and held his face.

"I can do that as many times as your face can take."

Elionor's cries waned. Raimond's vision spun—Damiano, Ago, Elionor.

The priest stood directly above. "The tavern's name is no longer relevant. Don't you think 'Two Burning Heretics' would better represent Chivasso?"

Raimond reached for him, but another kick landed on his chin.

Four men surrounded Raimond now. They bound his arms and stood him up.

Raimond glared at Ago. "Do what you must to me, but let Elionor live in peace. She won't burden anyone. Let her care for Damiano."

"That is Norma's choice, but I doubt she'll want the girl to be the slave of a weak, blind soldier."

"It's better than—"

Ago backhanded Raimond across the face. Raimond licked his lips as he staggered to keep his balance. Ago turned and left.

"You coward!" Damiano took a step and grasped the air. "Where are you, Ago?"

The priest snickered. "Go find him, blind man." He waved for the men. They pulled Raimond up and led him outside.

They dragged Raimond through the streets of Chivasso. The moon rose above the village; otherwise, blackness enveloped the houses, barns, and shops. A few villagers stepped outside, snickering and grinning, but as soon as Raimond passed, doors slammed shut. The glow from the looming bell tower cast an orange haze over the village square, and the Burning Heretic roared with jeers and laughter.

The men threw Raimond to the ground near the cathedral portal. "Lock him here," said the priest, sneering at Raimond.

Raimond glanced up and back, and there stood the same heavy stocks he had hidden behind the previous night.

The men lifted the top of the stocks and grabbed Raimond. He fought back, but after a few kicks to his side, he resigned himself to the inevitable. They jammed his feet into the stocks, replaced the top, and fastened it with a chain.

Last came a lock, which the priest dangled in front of Raimond. "Tomorrow Norma will introduce you to the whole village. And her mockery will be only the beginning, for not a single man, woman, child, or dog in Chivasso tolerates heretics."

7

Which executeth judgment for the oppressed: which giveth food to the hungry. The LORD looseth the prisoners.

—Psalm 146:7

A GUST OF FREEZING air blew into Raimond's shirt and ripped across his skin. His bones shivered and his jaw ached. His captors had fastened his legs between the two enormous blocks of wood. Leaning forward provided a little shelter from the wind, but as soon as his body warmed up, an ache formed in his back. So he leaned on his elbows until the cold forced him back up. It must be almost midnight, for the lantern in the bell tower no longer flung out its eerie light.

He breathed into the frigid air. His lungs burned, but he held in the coughs. Perhaps his final breaths would be in this village square. Then in heaven he could see Maria again—curly black hair, rosy face, and dimples in both cheeks. When Raimond had first believed the gospel, she hadn't rejected him. Less than a week later, she was a believer too.

Then, after years of waiting, came the joy of expecting a child. The months leading up to the birth were fraught with Maria's sickness and weakness, but the hope of a baby had kept her smiling. The night of the birth came—the midwife, the pain, the anticipation—but when the midwife spoke those horrible words, Raimond's entire life collapsed. Not only had his beloved wife died but so had their baby, Azalaïs, whose name Maria had chosen with her dying breaths. Becoming a barbe brought some relief from the pain, but the emptiness lingered.

A distant meow rippled through the night, and Raimond's mind went to Elionor. It had seemed so true and righteous—to adopt her, to raise her, to be her father. The hole that remained from Maria and Azalaïs seemed to finally be closing. Elionor was a glimmer of light in the shadows and a taste of hope amid sorrow.

But he had failed to rescue her and could do nothing for her here. Would she survive the next winter? Or perhaps she would endure her miserable childhood only to be ensnared by the sin that ruled this village.

How could a thirty-five-year-old itinerant preacher—hunted like a boar and despised like *la pesta*—raise a child? Now his life was in the hands of the Roman Catholic Church, and with no influential friends nearby, he could expect a long sentence in a dungeon, but more likely, torture and death. And Elionor was still trapped in Norma's snare.

Raimond scooted forward and wrapped his arms around his legs for what felt like the hundredth time. For some reason, God wanted him here in Chivasso at this moment. What was the Lord's grand design in his life, in Elionor's, in Damiano's? Norma had trodden over that blind and pitiful man as if he were dust on the road, and all for her own gain. Men like Damiano were littered throughout this realm—once vigorous men, now humiliated and cast aside like old rags. Yet they were often the men who listened to the gospel.

God had put Raimond in these stocks. Norma, the priest, or the men of Chivasso might think they had accomplished a great feat, but God alone had allowed it. Raimond rested his head on his knees.

"Lord, thank You for leading me to Elionor. I have seen Your works and Your power." He closed his eyes tightly. "But I have also failed You. You led me to Damiano, and instead of preaching the gospel, I denied my faith in You. I was afraid. Forgive me of my sin."

Whatever happened next, despite the guaranteed mocking and jeering, despite the certain humiliation, God would protect Elionor.

Raimond rested his face on his knees and closed his eyes. His muscles relaxed, and his pulse slowed to a steady thump. His last thoughts were singing with other believers in green mountain pastures, beautiful Maria, Azalaïs—and the outcast, Elionor.

Another gust of wind startled him awake, but this time Raimond breathed in the crisp air and relished it. God was present, and His sovereignty was perfect.

* * *

Swishing and shuffling awoke Raimond. He shivered and hugged his knees tighter, but the cold lingered. The sounds drifted nearer. He braced himself for the first eruption of ridicule and mockery.

All barbes knew what happened in situations like this. The people of Chivasso would likely pour all manner of filth on him; they would spill vile obscenities and throw curses. And that would all be before the inquisitor arrived and tried him.

Other than the shuffling sounds in the dark, the village square was silent. Even the light and laughter from the Burning Heretic were gone.

As Raimond scanned the square, two faint silhouettes swept from the shadows. Step by step, they moved toward him. Raimond sat straight and bolstered his courage.

The closer the silhouettes drew, the more they distinguished themselves. The shorter of the two walked in front of the taller one and guided him. Raimond rubbed his eyes and blinked. It was a child with frizzy hair and a man with a cane, carrying a bag over his shoulder.

Raimond shook his head rapidly and whispered, "You shouldn't be out here. Go home!"

Damiano tapped his cane on the ground and reached toward Raimond. "I will not let this happen to you, not while I'm alive and can breathe."

Raimond motioned toward the stocks. "You don't have the key, and these will be impossible to break."

"You are right about both options." Damiano set down his cane and allowed Elionor to place his hands on the stocks.

"If someone catches you here—"

"Before long, you and Elionor will be on the road west, and by the time Chivasso awakes, you'll be a league or more from here."

"There's nothing you can do for me," Raimond said. "I'm in the Lord's hands now."

Elionor ran to Raimond and threw both arms around him. "I want to go with you. No one else. I want to be your people, and I want you to be my babbo."

Raimond's heart sank as he hugged her. What she said was impossible. Even if he escaped the Church's wrath, he could never raise a girl by himself—not when God had called him to the ministry of preaching. "Elionor." Raimond caught her eyes and pointed at his feet. "Look at me. I wish that could happen, but it can't."

"What can't?" Damiano removed a small pouch from the bag slung over his shoulder and unwound the strap of leather that closed the pouch. "If Elionor was so courageous to sneak away from Norma tonight, if she was so intuitive to think of coming to me, if she was so persistent to beg me for help, couldn't you, Raimond Durand, a Vallense barbe of Valle dë Luserna, take her away from this horrible place and raise her as your own?"

"It's impossible. Perhaps if you could see—" Raimond caught himself and briskly shook his head. "Mi scusa, but what can a blind man and a child accomplish here?"

Damiano pulled a thin piece of metal about the length of a man's hand from the pouch. "If you would have listened to me earlier as intently as Elionor, perhaps you would know."

Raimond tilted his head.

"I might not see your ignorance, but I can feel it," Damiano said. "Is this your first time seeing a lockpick?"

"He's a blacksmith," Elionor said. "Don't you remember? Blacksmiths make locks, so I thought he could break one too."

"*Break* is perhaps not the right word, but I can probably unlock it without the key." Damiano held his hand toward Elionor. "Take me to the lock, cita."

"You can't see it," Raimond said. "I don't intend to be rude, but have you tried this since you lost your sight?"

"I've hidden in that old house far too long, letting Norma and Ago dictate my every action. No longer." As soon as Elionor put his hands on the lock, Damiano explored it with his fingers. "Ah, it's a strong chain. And good iron." He rubbed his fingers on the keyhole. "This will require both time and patience."

Raimond rubbed his cheek. "Can you break it off instead?"

"And wake all of Chivasso?" Damiano chuckled as he inserted the pick into the keyhole. "Besides, do you know a few men who would help carry an anvil to this spot? I thought not. Now let me work." He wiggled the pick for a moment before holding it out toward Elionor. "I need one with a smaller hook on the end. Do you see it?"

Elionor took the larger pick from Damiano. "I can't see these. It's too dark."

"Use the fingertips God gave you. They're just as useful as those eyes of yours."

Soon Elionor held out another pick for Damiano, which he inserted into the keyhole and oscillated. "Two levers." He continued to tinker as his breaths grew shorter.

Raimond leaned toward his knees and observed. There was nothing like watching a man of expertise. Far in the distance, a door slammed. A gust of wind hit Raimond's cheek. "Why risk your life to free a Vallense like me from the stocks?"

"This lever is tougher than poison." Damiano tapped the lock with his fingers, grimaced, and slumped. "So you admit who you are now? But to answer your question, I want to do something good for once. Something that lasts longer than a day."

"By helping a heretic?"

Damiano took a deep breath and inserted a pick into the lock again. "I have experienced more hatred and bloodshed than any man should. I was on God's side, I thought, as I stabbed a Turk and watched him die. And the Turks thought the same as they sliced my friend Vilfred across the chest. How could God cause men to hate and kill? It's exactly what the priest and the Church want to do to you too. When the child came to me, begging me to use the skills I long ago forsook, I couldn't refuse." The lock clicked, and Damiano smiled. "That was one lever, and now for this other one."

"Come to the mountains with us. We'll welcome you there and care for your needs. I could do no less after what you've done here."

"A blind killer? A crusader? Do you know what else I've done in my years? I would make any Vallense blush. Maybe you're generous, but others won't feel the same. Elionor, though—I think Vilfred would have wanted a Vallense to raise her."

"He was a leader in the Order of the Holy Cross, you said. He hunted us."

"Seeing the horrors of war changed him. It did the same to me but in different ways. Some of what he said, you might be surprised—"

The lock clicked again. Damiano pulled the shackle up and unlatched it from the chain. Elionor struggled to pull the chain from its loops until Damiano lent his strength. He lifted the top of the stocks from Raimond's legs.

"Damiano, come with us. I will tell you about the Savior—"

"Take me home before you depart, për piasì. I'll manage Norma if she's bold enough to confront me."

Raimond stood, but lightheadedness pulsed through him. He placed a hand on the stocks to catch himself and stretched but kept both eyes alert. "Norma will hunt us, and we won't be safe anywhere in Piedmont. If I take Elionor, all the rumors about Vallenses stealing children will be true."

"Trust me, Raimond, I won't allow Norma to harm you. She fears me and what I know about her brother."

"Then I can't let anyone find you helping me here." Raimond grabbed Damiano's arm with one hand and held Elionor with the other. His wobbly legs made walking a struggle, but by the time they exited the square, his head was clear and his stride was sure.

Before they left Chivasso, Elionor was asleep on Raimond's shoulder. The river's rushing grew louder the closer they drew to Damiano's barn. When they arrived, Raimond gave Elionor a pat on the back. "We're missing your companion."

Elionor opened one eye and yawned. "Who?"

"Rosmarin, of course!" Raimond let Elionor down and turned to Damiano. "There's so much I want to tell you."

"I understand, and perhaps someday we will meet again. My one request is that you always choose what is best for Elionor."

Raimond put his hand over his heart and bowed his head. "I will."

Elionor walked to Damiano and hugged him. "Mersì for helping me."

A coarse laugh suddenly bellowed from the road behind them, scraping Raimond's eardrums like a gritty stone. "Saint Joseph, you rat! I found you!"

8

The LORD openeth the eyes of the blind: the LORD raiseth them that are bowed down: the LORD loveth the righteous.

—Psalm 146:8

DAMIANO FLUNG HIS hands into the air toward Raimond. "Go now, across the bridge and to the mountains. I'll distract Norma."

Another shout rippled through the black air. Norma strutted into view, bearing a torch. With her were three men. One carried a knife and bared his teeth like a rabid hound, while another held a thick stick. The priest who had arrested Raimond scowled as he held aloft a processional crucifix. Rosmarin hissed and leaped from Elionor's arms.

Raimond lifted Elionor and grabbed Damiano's arm. "You're coming with us. I won't leave you with these people."

Damiano pulled away. "They can't do anything to me. I know too much, and if they—"

"I told you to never meddle in my affairs, Damiano Rivera." Norma took a few steps in front of the men with her. "Since you've chosen the heretic's side, you'll see what it feels like to be alone and abandoned, and now without a servant to keep you from tripping over your own feet."

Damiano frowned, and his breathing became heavy. "You liar. How dare you speak to me after what you have done to your own niece."

Raimond scanned the men flanking Norma. The priest might wear an elaborate robe, but his stance was as strong as a miner. The other men looked like grizzled tavern dwellers whom Raimond might best individually but not together. This was a confrontation he couldn't win with words or weapons. He slid his hand down to Damiano's wrist and latched on. "We leave now."

With one arm holding Elionor and his other hand on Damiano's arm, Raimond lunged into a run. But Damiano's steps were cautious, his posture unsteady. If it were only Elionor, Raimond could escape, but with Damiano—

He had to try. Damiano needed someone to care for him. He needed a purpose. He needed the salvation offered through Jesus Christ. Raimond pressed through the aching of his spine and the burning of his muscles as he kept Damiano from falling into the snow. Footsteps pounded behind him, but he locked his gaze on the cobblestone arch ahead of him.

A tall man stood in the middle of the bridge. His feet were spread, his hands on his hips, though his face was anything but determined. *Ago.*

Damiano suddenly ripped his arm free from Raimond, bent over, and placed his hands on his knees. "I can't . . . I can't breathe. I need . . ." He wheezed as if his throat were smaller than a keyhole.

Ago slunk forward, shoulders slumping. Elionor clung to Raimond like ivy on stone.

Raimond turned back toward their pursuers. No more than fifteen paces away, Norma stood with the priest and two men.

"Trapped!" Norma spat on the road and wiped her mouth. "You're not the first Vallense I've captured." She cackled. "Don't ask me his name. All I know is we threw his ashes into the Po, as we'll soon do to you, Saint Joseph." She looked at Elionor and waved. "Come with me, maraja. This heretic wants to boil you, eat you, and throw your bones to his dogs."

Elionor buried her face in Raimond's shoulder. "She lies! She always lies!"

"Indeed, a liar." Damiano stepped forward, still wheezing. "Do your friends here know about Vilfred?"

"Vilfred was the founder of our . . ." Norma shot a glance at Raimond.

"I know everything, and so do others," Damiano said. "All your work in Piedmont will be revealed, and thus will your efforts in Piedmont be dismantled."

"You would side with a heretic?"

"I side with justice and with the man who showed compassion for Vilfred's child, whom you have rejected and despised. I don't know if God sides with the Roman Church or with the Vallenses, but I do know He is against you, Norma Bifano."

Her face turned crimson. "Stand aside or suffer the same fate as the heretic."

"No one knows about your brother, do they? They don't know what he said while he lay dying on the battlefield."

"Silence!" Norma took a step toward Damiano.

"I've been silent for too long—too many months of lingering in darkness while you wove your lies through this village. No more."

Raimond glanced back toward the bridge and whispered, "Ago is behind us. We're surrounded."

Damiano spun toward the bridge. "Ago, Ago. I pulled you from the streets, gave you an honest wage, provided you a room in my home, and now you align yourself with Norma." He shook his head. "All for the few coins she was willing to part with. I thought you were a better man. Look at Elionor and tell me you pity her. Do you? I may not see the child, but you—you have watched her deteriorate, nò? And now you stand between the girl and her one hope of avoiding a life as miserable as Norma's."

Ago's hands shook as he stepped to the side.

"Stand your ground!" Norma shouted.

Ago stared at the stones beneath him. "I didn't, I mean, I couldn't have known—"

"That you would allow a little girl to starve? That you would take the money meant for her and give it to the most wretched woman in Chivasso? Does your mother whom you claim to support know about this?" Damiano held out his hand. "Për piasì, Ago, take this chance to redeem yourself."

Ago glanced at Norma, then at Elionor and Raimond, and

paused on Damiano. "Forgive me, Maestro." He lowered his chin and held his hands together. "I beg you, forgive me."

Damiano pushed Raimond toward the bridge. "Go while you have a chance."

Raimond stood his ground. "I won't leave without you."

"You can't outrun us." Norma's voice was quick but unsure. "We'll find you wherever you hide. The whole realm will know you stole a Catholic child from her family. Every village in Piedmont will know your name, and you'll never rest."

Damiano reached beneath his shirt and removed a small bundle of parchment. "These are Vilfred's signed wishes, and somewhere in here is his statement that I am Elionor's protector." He fumbled the papers as he handed them to Raimond. "Find that note, and there you will also find his testimony about the Order of the Holy Cross—the leaders, the villages where they are active, and the people they suspect are Vallenses."

"Lies, lies, lies." Norma crossed her arms. "Every one of them lies."

Raimond held up a sheet of parchment and strained to read it. The words were scribbled, and he couldn't discern any of them in the darkness.

"And most important of all," Damiano said, "are Vilfred's notes about the Vallenses. Listen now, men."

"Nò! Don't listen to him!" Norma pointed at Raimond and Damiano. "Drag them to the stocks!"

The priest strode forward, but the two other men hesitated.

"Vilfred sympathized with Vallense teachings," Damiano said. "As he neared death, he questioned not only the Order of the Holy Cross but the whole edifice of the Catholic Church—the priesthood, the pope, all of it. As he drew his last breath, I wondered if he had accepted the Vallense religion. After all the years hunting Vallenses, after all the wrath he tried to pour upon them, he might very well have become one himself."

The priest grabbed the man with the knife and pulled him forward. "Silence that man!"

Norma shoved the man in the back. "And throw the maraja into the river!"

Raimond gripped Elionor tightly as he backed away onto the bridge.

"I'll lock you in the stocks with the heretic preacher!" The priest pushed the second man forward, but he refused to budge. "Take him and the blind man immediately."

Norma kicked the man's legs. "Move, you fat boars!"

The man with the knife faced the priest. "This is your fight, not mine."

"Fight these enemies of Christ and receive your salvation!"

"By throwing a little girl into the river? I don't think God would want that. Besides, the tavern is calling my name." The man shook his head and turned back toward the village. The priest swung the crucifix at him, but the man stepped out of reach. He began walking away, and the other man joined him.

The priest raised the crucifix. "The entire parish will know of your treachery!"

The men didn't acknowledge the shouting and continued walking until they passed into the shadows.

Norma's shoulders rose and fell. She stormed toward Damiano and lifted her hands as if she wanted to strangle him. "This is your fault!"

Damiano's breath grew labored. "Nò, all the turmoil here is your doing. It is you who forsook your duty to care for Elionor. Vilfred—"

"Is dead, and he was a fool for allowing himself to be killed. Vilfred was the last of my family. And look at your pitiful self." Norma smacked the blind man's ear and laughed. "You felt that, but what can you do about it?"

Raimond flinched and let Elionor down but still held her hand tightly.

Norma stepped to the side and hit Damiano on the back of the head. "Imprisoned in your own mind without a key to unlock the chains. Do something! Hit me back!"

Damiano reared back his arm and swung wide, but all he connected with was air.

Norma belted out a laugh. "Return to your gloomy house and sit in your chair, you miserable man. You should've died in battle like Vilfred instead of living like this. At least then people would call you a hero instead of a beast."

Damiano jabbed, but Norma took a step to the right and avoided him.

"Stand back, Norma," Raimond called. "You're defeated."

Norma grabbed her own hair, pulled it, and screeched. She threw herself at Damiano, slapping, spitting, and biting with the hatred of a demon. Damiano tried to walk backward and block her, yet every blow came with such a vengeance that he couldn't defend himself.

Raimond released Elionor's hand and pointed to the opposite side of the bridge. "I'll find you there after I help him."

Elionor scurried away. Raimond turned back toward Damiano and Norma. His breath fled.

At the precipice of the icy river, Norma held Damiano in a headlock, struggling to heave him into the rapids. She kicked the back of his legs, pounded a fist into his cheek, and finally bit his shoulder. Raimond sprinted toward them, ready to fling Norma into the snow.

Near the edge, Damiano swayed and lost his footing. Norma grabbed his shoulders and threw him over the side. But Damiano still held her arm, and into the river fell Norma too.

Raimond glanced toward Elionor to be sure she was safe, ran down the bridge, and jumped in to save Damiano's life.

9

The LORD preserveth the strangers; he relieveth the fatherless and widow: but the way of the wicked he turneth upside down.

—Psalm 146:9

THE SHOCK OF the water stole Raimond's breath, his vision, and his sense of touch. His legs flailed, his lungs refusing to expand. He found the river bottom and straightened enough to raise his head above water as the current pressed against him.

The bridge loomed above him. Downstream, silhouettes of boulders stood above the rapids like sentinels. He gasped, and though it wasn't much of a breath, it was enough to gain focus.

If he didn't escape this torrent soon, he would be dead. And so would Damiano.

Raimond marked the place where Damiano had fallen and pushed himself into deeper water.

The raging current propelled him into the shadows. Something hard slammed against his knee, spinning him around and pressing him into a boulder. He grasped for a handhold, a ledge, anything to steady himself.

At last he found the corner of a flat rock and pulled himself from the current. *Please, Lord, let me find him.*

A wave hit Raimond, and he shook his head vigorously. He tried to wipe the water from his eyes, but the blurs and shadows clouded his vision. His chest heaved. He craned his neck, and a dark shape caught his eye. Pressed against a nearby boulder, water rushing around him, was Damiano.

Raimond crashed back into the current, but it swept him downstream. He forced his head above water and reached deep into his soul for strength. He pushed through the tide and plunged toward Damiano.

As his strength faded, his eyesight dimmed, and all he heard was the splash of water in his ears. Then his feet touched bottom.

Raimond stood and gasped. He was under the bridge, so Damiano must be close. He clawed his way around the rocks and into the shallows, but the more his body was exposed, the more he shook.

He climbed onto a rock. Though the breeze might be gentle, it felt more violent than the raging torrent. He crawled onto another rock, and there below him was Damiano, his body half submerged in the water.

Raimond grabbed Damiano's arms and heaved him up onto the rock.

He leaned over Damiano. "Can you hear me? Damiano! Damiano!"

There was no answer, but light puffs of air streamed from the man's nostrils.

"The riverbank is nearby. I'm taking you there. All will be well."

Raimond scanned the waters for any signs of Norma but found nothing except white rapids and rocks. If she wasn't here, then the river had taken her under—a miserable end for a miserable person.

He lifted Damiano off the rock and stepped into the knee-deep water. This time the water didn't shock him, for now the breeze was his tormentor. He waded through the shallows until the water was only ankle deep. At last he climbed onto the bank. He laid Damiano on the dry gravel and collapsed.

But he couldn't stay there. They needed a fire. And Elionor—he had to find her.

Raimond rose, and as if beyond the confines of earth, he lifted Damiano and carried him up the embankment and onto the road.

"Monsù!" Elionor's desperate plea rose above the commotion of the river. "Help!"

At the far end of the bridge, a light flickered. Elionor's voice rose again but broke off. Raimond struggled toward the blurry glow, his chest tight.

The robed priest now held a torch instead of the crucifix. Norma stood beside him, clasping Elionor with both arms. Water dripped from Norma's hair and streamed over a new wound on the side of her head. Her savage eyes fell on Raimond as Elionor kicked and flailed.

Raimond knelt and laid Damiano on the ground. "I'll return in a moment, my friend."

Rising, Raimond glared at Norma. His clothes were drenched, his skin numb and bones stiff. But he flexed his fingers, set his jaw, and marched across the bridge.

"Release Elionor now. You've caused enough harm tonight, Norma Bifano. I won't allow you to cause more."

"Do you see me standing here? I can't die. Damiano couldn't kill me, the river couldn't kill me, and neither can you. The maraja is mine now that the blind fool is dead."

Raimond pulled up his soaked sleeves and squared his shoulders. "Come no closer, you spiteful ghost of Saint Joseph. Stop!"

He didn't stop.

Norma wrapped an arm around Elionor's neck. "I'll . . . I'll choke her. I promise you I will. Better she dies and goes to her babbo than a Vallense snatch her." She tightened her arm, enough to lift Elionor's feet off the ground.

The priest threw his torch into the river, raised both fists, and blocked Raimond. "In the name of Christ and the Blessed Virgin, surrender or face our wrath."

Raimond shoved the priest aside and kept his focus on Norma. "Let her go."

The priest pivoted into Raimond's path and swung a right hook.

Raimond spread his feet and turned his shoulder, easily absorbing the punch. His own jab landed directly on the priest's nose. He followed with a hard right cross to the man's temple.

The priest stood stunned for a moment. Then his eyes rolled back. He collapsed into a heap of robes.

Raimond gave his arms a quick shake, sidestepped the priest, and advanced toward Norma.

No sound came from Elionor as she squirmed—not a whimper, not a plea, not a cry—but her eyes begged for help. Then came a desperate gasp for air.

Raimond grabbed Norma under the chin with one hand and pried her arm from Elionor's neck with the other.

Elionor held her throat and wheezed, then found refuge behind Raimond.

He glanced over the side of the bridge as he locked both hands around Norma's neck . Throwing her over would be simple. She would no longer be a threat to Elionor, him, or any other Vallense.

He might have done it in his angry youth, but the gospel of Jesus Christ had changed him. He tossed Norma against the cobblestone parapet.

Norma snarled, staggered up, and lowered her shoulder. She charged at him like a wild beast.

Raimond wheeled to the side, and she rammed into the knee-high parapet. She shrieked and tumbled over the parapet. The blunt impact below made Raimond flinch.

He ran to the parapet and searched the water. There amid the shallows floated Norma's broken, lifeless body. A violent wave seized it and carried it downstream. He looked away, his heart thumping, his breath coming in rhythmic pants. He turned his back and lifted Elionor into his arms.

Elionor threw her arms around him. "I couldn't see you in the water, Monsù! Then Magna found me, and I ran, and then the priest caught me—"

"But God saved both of us. 'For the LORD your God is he that goeth with you, to fight for you against your enemies, to save you.'"

"What about Monsù Damiano? Will God save him too?"

"A fire. Can you go to Damiano's hearth and stoke the fire?"

She pressed her lips together, nodded, and ran toward the nearby villa with Rosmarin following close behind.

Raimond knelt beside Damiano and listened for his breath. It was fleeting, but still there.

Step by step, Raimond carried Damiano's limp and broken body to the villa. The warm air inside brought the tingling pain of a thousand needle pricks over his body. His vision blurred as he entered the room where Damiano had earlier hosted them. Elionor prodded the logs with a rod, and the fire roared.

Raimond laid Damiano on the floor near the hearth, removed his drenched clothing, and covered him in blankets. Damiano's arms felt like ice, yet he didn't shiver. "Blankets, për piasì. We need more. And dry clothes."

Elionor ran into the hallway. Raimond removed his own wet clothing, wrapped himself in the last blanket, and sat as close to the fire as he could.

A whisper came from Damiano, but it was too faint for Raimond to discern the words.

He leaned over and touched Damiano's brow. "Are you awake? Did you say something?"

Damiano's hollow eyes stared up at the ceiling as he gave the slightest nod.

"Are you comfortable? Is the fire too warm?"

"I . . . I'm dying."

"Nò, you're warming. You'll live."

Damiano wheezed.

Raimond opened Damiano's blanket and felt the man's chest. It rose and fell, but only slightly. Then he felt the broken ribs.

"Remember, always choose what is best for Elionor." Damiano's chest trembled under the strain of speaking. "I've fulfilled my vow . . . to Vilfred."

Raimond's throat tightened. "Your soul—it's more important than your vow. Don't leave this world uncertain about eternity."

Damiano smiled with one side of his mouth. "Now you preach to me."

"Jesus died and was resurrected so you might have God's forgiveness. Even at this late hour—"

"I . . . I know. My sins I forsake. My faith is in . . . my Savior. And Elionor, give her . . ."

Damiano breathed out, but he didn't breathe again.

Tears streamed down Raimond's cheeks as he closed Damiano's eyes. Soon Elionor returned and covered both Damiano and Raimond in more blankets. But Raimond didn't have the strength to tell her about Damiano—not yet.

Unrolling the clothes he had shed, he removed the little box from the pocket and opened it. The outside was wet, but the wax-coated flowers inside were as cheerful as ever. He lay down beside the hearth, and a moment later, Rosmarin brushed along his side, meowed, and curled up against his chest. The fire crackled as Raimond drifted off to sleep.

10

A ROOSTER'S CROW PULLED Raimond from his slumber. Faint sunlight glowed from the hall. He turned to the side, and reality flooded back into his mind at the sight of Damiano's lifeless body. The village would soon awaken, and Raimond and Elionor were far from safe.

Raimond scanned the room for Elionor and found her curled up with Rosmarin on the far side of the hearth. He needed to bury Damiano before she awoke. A pile of clothing lay on the table, exactly as Raimond had asked Elionor.

His knee buckled when he stood, sending a tingle up his back. He closed his eyes, sighed, and waited for the pain to subside before he left the room and changed into the dry clothes.

He crept back into the dining room, picked up the body, and carried it outside. Damiano deserved a proper burial, despite the danger that might soon befall them. Raimond found a shovel in the barn, then a spot of soft ground under a beech tree.

Each time Raimond stuck the shovel into the hardened winter earth, he ached, not so much from the physical pain as from the tragic end of Damiano's existence—blind, beguiled, and rejected, with no one to do better than take advantage of him. Like soot swept from a hearth, men like Damiano were often forgotten, waiting for the wind to carry them away. Elionor needed a man like Raimond to rescue her, but so did men like Damiano.

Sweat beaded on Raimond's brow. He lowered the body into the hole and covered it. What could he do? What could he say to honor a man like this?

Elionor appeared from around the corner of the villa, carrying Rosmarin and yawning. "What are you doing?"

Raimond glanced down at the grave and stuck the shovel in the ground, but her narrowed eyes revealed her ignorance.

"Monsù Damiano. He couldn't . . ." Raimond motioned for Elionor, and when she was close, he lifted her and Rosmarin into his arms. "I buried him here this morning."

"Can we pray for him to go to God?"

"He's already with God, just like my wife and baby girl. The Holy Scriptures promise Damiano would go to God if he believed on Christ, and he did last night. For that we can rejoice."

A few tears dropped from Elionor's eyes. She pulled Rosmarin close and held her cheek against the cat's fur. "Can we leave now?"

Bug-ridden hair, dirt-smudged skin, tattered clothing, and a hungry stomach—where would he begin? The villa's pantry would hold some food, but a child in her state needed a steady diet before she would be healthy again. What then? Could Raimond be a father to her? Was it time to settle into the life of a Vallense farmer again—to plow a barley field, build a stone fence, plant and reap a harvest?

It all seemed so virtuous and comforting—a welcome fulfillment for all the loss he had seen. Yet meeting Elionor and Damiano had further confirmed his divine calling to the outcasts of this world. He wouldn't forsake that calling.

Raimond pushed the future back to where it belonged and set Elionor on her feet. "Sì, we'll leave as soon as we eat."

The sun stood at its zenith when Raimond and Elionor struck the path west. The sky was too dreary for Raimond to pick out the mountains, but Elionor and Rosmarin still walked with a bounce. Elionor never once looked back at Chivasso as she held Raimond's hand, marching off to a new home and a new life.

But what role would Raimond take in that life?

* * *

Two days of walking brought Raimond and Elionor into the valleys of the mighty Alps. They trudged through knee-deep snow on a path made by the footsteps of others. A few times, Raimond had to carry Elionor and Rosmarin. As they passed through the Vallense hamlet of Luserna, Raimond greeted a friend and held a brief conversation.

Elionor tilted her head to the side after they were done. "Why were your words so strange?"

"We were speaking in our tongue, Romaunt. It's like your Piedmontese, but I imagine it's odd to you. For example, instead of saying *sì* as you do, we say *òc*."

"What did you say to that man?"

"First I said *bonjorn*. That means 'hello.' He asked me where I was going, and I told him Valon de Rorà—the Deep Valley of Rorà." Raimond pointed to the right at a cut in the mountain wall. "I know a family up there who will have room to spare for us."

"Will they let me sleep in their house?"

"For certain."

Up they climbed into the Rorà Valley, forging their way through wintery oak forests and high alpine pastures. The snow grew deeper and the path less trodden, so Raimond carried Elionor on his shoulders and held Rosmarin in his arms. His muscles ached, and the icy wind was relentless, but up here they were safe from all who meant them harm.

They crested one last steep ridge. Downhill, nestled into a hillside, stood a humble stone house with a trail of smoke streaming from its chimney. After they wound down the short trail to the house, Raimond set Elionor on the doorstep and knocked.

The door swung open, and warm air rolled out. Raimond closed his eyes for a moment to take it in.

"Who is . . . *Monsen* Raimond! And who is this?" Magdalena Janavel grabbed Raimond by the arm and pulled him toward the door. "Come in and warm yourselves."

Raimond stepped into the house while Elionor grabbed Rosmarin and rushed to the hearth. Linen curtains divided the home into three rooms, and timber rafters vaulted the ceiling to a spacious height.

Lambert Janavel rose from a chair, holding a newborn lamb. "*Bonser*, old friend. What brings you to our valley?"

Magdalena ran to the fire, grabbed a poker, and stirred the embers. "Water—we need water from the well. And surely we could roast a chicken for our guests too. You will stay here tonight, Monsen Raimond. Lambert says a snowstorm is brewing in the heights."

"Your hospitality is legendary." Raimond found a place near the fire and held his hands toward the flames. "We'll eat whatever you can spare."

Lambert walked over to Elionor and bent to her level. "*Cossí te dison?*"

Elionor glanced up at Raimond and squinted.

"This is Monsen Lambert Janavel. He asked what your name is, so you can say '*Me dison . . .*'"

"Elionor!" she said, smiling.

Lambert raised his chin. "Piedmontese?"

Raimond nodded. "She's from the plains—Chivasso to be exact."

"Dear, sweet child." Magdalena pressed her skirts in, sat beside Elionor, and examined the girl's hair. "Soon you will have a warm bath, and you will be cleaner than a fresh snowfall." She leaned toward her husband and whispered, "The water?"

Lambert stood straight and bowed slightly to Elionor. "I draw the purest, clearest water in all the realm from my well."

"But you won't want to sit in it until it's warm, which will take some time." Magdalena sighed. "So much to do."

"I'll prepare the chicken," Raimond said. "Is there one in particular?"

"We'll do that while you two rest. You look as though today has lasted a week." Magdalena smiled at Elionor and petted the cat. "What's his name?"

After Raimond translated, Elionor gave a little laugh. "Rosmarin is a girl!"

"*Perdon!*" Magdalena leaned down and looked Rosmarin in the eye. "How dare I insult such a pretty girl."

Elionor giggled before Raimond could translate. Words and pronunciations might vary, but feelings were universal.

By sunset, Magdalena had prepared a full barrel of warm water. Meanwhile, Lambert butchered the chicken, and after Magdalena seasoned it, he stuck it on a spit to roast over the fire. The aromas from the chicken made Raimond's mouth water. Laughter and splashes poured out from the adjoining room where Magdalena bathed Elionor.

While Raimond recounted the story about Chivasso, Elionor, Norma, and Damiano, Lambert sat at the hearth and rotated the spit. "So you will raise the girl as your own? I can't think of a more deserving man, but still, I have yet to hear about an unmarried barbe adopting a child, especially one so young."

"Part of me wants to be a father again. God put me in Elionor's path for His purpose, and for a time, I thought that purpose was to be her father. I also thought she could help fill that lingering emptiness from . . ." Raimond stared at the floor. "When Maria and Azalaïs died, I committed myself to ministry. I have no house, no land to farm, no wife. Raising Elionor might be fulfilling, but I believe God wants so much more for her. And me. In these dark days, the world needs men to find wandering sheep like Damiano. And Elionor needs more than I can offer."

Lambert picked up the poker and moved the embers. "You brought her to my home for a reason."

"We've been friends for years, Lambert. You were one of the men who helped me most when my family died. You also encouraged me when I committed myself to being a barbe." Raimond reached into his pocket and removed the immortèlas. "Magdalena picked these flowers and preserved them in wax so I could remember Maria and Azalaïs. I can't imagine a better couple to approach, but I would never impose."

"Impose a child?" Lambert's shoulders bounced as he chuckled. "I'm surprised you would be willing to part with such a sweet girl."

"I know it's right." Raimond turned his head toward the laughter streaming from the other room. Damiano wanted him to always choose what was best for Elionor, and more than that, God's will and His ways reigned over all. "Elionor needs a mother." He caught Lambert's eyes. "And a steadfast father."

"I don't know what to say. We've been praying for years, and here I am in my fortieth year."

Raimond took over the spit and turned it. Juices dripped onto the fire, bringing a sharp sizzle and rich fragrance to the air. "Perhaps Elionor is God's answer. Speak to Magdalena about it."

"I already know what she'll say!" Lambert stood, put his hands on his head, and grinned. "I'm going to tell her."

"Let me tell Elionor, though."

"Tell me what?" Elionor stepped from behind the curtain, wearing a billowing shirt and skirts twice the length they needed to be. Her hair had been cut nearly to the scalp, but that didn't steal the joy from her countenance.

Magdalena stepped beside her. "These clothes were all I could find. I'm afraid Elionor's old clothes are beyond their days of usefulness, even for stuffing a mattress. I have spare linen, though, and given a few days, I could sew a dress more fitting. How long will you be staying?"

Raimond eyed Lambert. "Not long."

"I had to cut off all Ellie's hair."

"Ellie?" Raimond raised his brows at Elionor.

"I like that name. But I still like Elionor too." She touched the crown of her head. "*Madòna* Magdalena said it will grow back soon. And it won't itch anymore. I want it to grow all the way to the floor!"

"You said *madòna*. Do you speak Romaunt now?"

"I know *madòna* and *madomaisèla* and *monsen*."

"*Excellenta!* Before long, you'll be speaking better than I do!"

Elionor patted her leg, and Rosmarin bounded up into her arms. "May I bathe Rosmarin?" she asked in Piedmontese.

Raimond translated, and Magdalena answered. "Certainly, but first you must eat."

As they sat around the table, Raimond recounted tales of lands far over the mountains and the small churches he had visited. Magdalena and Lambert tried to include Elionor in the conversation, which resulted in her giggling at their feeble attempts to speak

Piedmontese. When they had eaten the meal and cleared the table, Magdalena helped Elionor bathe Rosmarin and finally bundled them both onto a mat in the adjoining room. Lambert then took his wife to another room.

Raimond sat near the fire and read the notes Damiano had given him. The Order of the Holy Cross had indeed woven its web wide. On the first page were places: Turin, Pinerolo, Saint Ambrogio, and many more. The next page held what must have been the names of informants or leaders. Most were Piedmontese, but one name caught his attention—Chanforan. Raimond had once heard of a pastor in Turin with that name, but he had disgraced himself years ago and had recently died. Raimond shrugged and continued sifting through the parchment. This information would help the barbes be more cautious when ministering in certain places.

Soon Lambert returned with Magdalena at his side. "Are you certain Elionor wants this?" Magdalena asked Raimond, tears streaming down her cheeks.

"She might not realize it yet, but I know it will be best for her, for you, and for me." Raimond looked at them both. "All I ask is that you raise her in the truth we all hold dear. Show her the way to the Savior and His forgiveness. Give her a new life, free from the pain she would have been enslaved to."

Lambert held Magdalena's arm and stood tall. "With God's help, and by the love of Christ that constrains us, we will."

Raimond let out a long sigh. "Then I'll tell her in the morning."

* * *

The wind howled that night, but barely a draft penetrated the stone and plaster walls beside Raimond's pallet. Lambert had built this house well. He was a good man, and he would be the perfect papà for Elionor. Before dawn, he went outside and returned with an armful of chopped wood. He stomped the snow from his boots, and as he rekindled the fire, Magdalena hung a kettle on one of the pothooks.

Raimond stood and stretched. "I will leave this morning."

"*Non*, please stay longer," Lambert said. "A blanket of snow fell last night, so the trek down to Luserna will be difficult."

Raimond laughed. "It won't be the first time I've trudged through snow. Last week when I crossed the Great Saint Bernard Pass, the drifts were up to my hips."

"Why leave so soon?" Magdalena asked.

Little feet plodded on the floor, and a cat meowed from behind the curtain. Elionor yawned as she stepped out, cradling Rosmarin. "May we stay longer?" she asked in a sleepy tone.

Raimond glanced at Lambert and Magdalena. Then he sat in a chair and waved Elionor to him. "You will stay here with Monsen Lambert and Madòna Magdalena, and they will be your babbo and mima."

Elionor opened her mouth and stared at the Janavels but froze in place.

"They are good people, as you have seen, and they—"

"I want to go with you, Monsen Raimond!" Elionor's chin quivered, and her voice shook. She set Rosmarin down and threw herself into his arms. "I want to go with you!"

Raimond patted Elionor's back and took a deep breath to hold back the tears. "I know, but look at them. Look at them, Elionor. You'll have not only a *papà* but also a *mamà*. And you need both." He rubbed her short strands of hair. "I wouldn't have known to cut your hair. Mothers know things like this."

Magdalena wiped her eyes and let out a sound that resembled both a cry and a laugh. Lambert walked closer and bent down to Elionor. "We would be delighted to call you our daughter."

"I know it's hard to understand." Raimond wiped a tear from her eye. "Do you remember when you were scared of Monsù Damiano?"

Elionor gave a few abrupt nods.

"What did I tell you then?"

"Not to be afraid. And that not knowing the future is a gift."

"Sì, a gift from God, and I would tell you the same now, dear Elionor. I love you, and that's why I brought you out of Chivasso— to this land, to this people, and to this family. Most important of all, I know Lambert and Magdalena will care for your soul. They'll instruct you in the Holy Scriptures, they'll teach you right from wrong, they'll introduce you to Jesus Christ, who died on the cross to save you from your sins." Raimond peered over Elionor's shoulder at the door. "And while they love and teach you here, I must do the same for others out there. They haven't had the privilege of the upbringing you'll know here—one I would have given everything for at your age."

The fire crackled, but otherwise all was silent. Raimond swallowed and wiped another tear from Elionor's cheek.

She smiled slightly and did the same for him. "I'm not afraid anymore."

"I've never known a girl with so much courage. And I will never forget this little girl from Chivasso."

Elionor threw her arms around Raimond's neck. "I won't forget you either."

She might not forget Raimond, but as years passed, the details from the last four days would grow foggy. That would be better, though. Her childhood memories should be filled with Magdalena's laughter and Lambert's stoic yet gentle care, not Norma's vile words.

With Elionor still latching on to him, Raimond stood and walked to Lambert and Magdalena. Elionor lifted her head, and Magdalena held out her arms. "We love you, Ellie."

Raimond gave Elionor a nod and a wink.

"What about Rosmarin?" Elionor widened her eyes and looked at the Janavels. "Can she be in our family too?"

"Of course!" Magdalena laughed, and Elionor jumped from Raimond's arms into hers.

Standing back, Raimond watched as Lambert and Magdalena hugged and kissed their new daughter. Her smile revealed a contentment deeper than the roots of the mountains. Soon the scant language barrier would melt like snow in spring, and Elionor would be more Vallense than Piedmontese.

Raimond gathered his few belongings, strapped on his shoes, and donned his hat.

"Stay with us, at least until the Sunday gathering," Magdalena said. "God blessed us with a good harvest, and our stores are full."

"There's nowhere I would rather stay than here, but I wouldn't be content for long. My service to God and His calling compels me to new lands and new people."

Lambert set Elionor on her feet. "You will always be welcome in our home."

Raimond opened his arms and embraced Elionor one last time. "God has used you, Elionor, and for that I will be forever grateful. Now I want to help people more than ever before."

"Where will you go next?" Magdalena asked.

"First to Val Angrogna for a personal matter. Then I'll cross the mountains to Savoy, though the place doesn't matter. I want to find men like Damiano, wherever they may be, before it's too late for them—not the respectable ones, but the forsaken sons, the stumbling drunks, and the blind soldiers. They need to believe in the Savior too." Raimond knelt and looked at Elionor. "*Adieu*, mi amis Elionor Janavel. Obey your babbo and mima."

"Papà and mamà, you mean." Her wide smile unveiled two dimples on her cheeks.

"Indeed, papà and mamà."

The alpine wind blew in as soon as Raimond opened the door. After a parting greeting from the Janavels and a low bow to Rosmarin, Raimond turned and found the winding path.

Every step through the snow propelled him farther into his renewed calling and purpose. Though the wind howled and frigid air pricked his skin, his heart was warm, his mind clear, his soul fulfilled.

Late that afternoon, he climbed a ridge overlooking Val Angrogna and found the knoll he often visited. The weather was calmer here than in the Rorà Valley, and the sun cast a brilliant light on two engraved stones. One said MARIA and the other BABY GIRL. Raimond opened the little box and smiled back at the two immortèlas. Someday, his body would likely be laid to rest at this gravesite, but until then, God would be both his comfort and his strength.

Raimond gently closed the box and gazed at the mountains towering above him. Threads of chimney smoke streamed upward from the scores of houses far below. These valleys were truly an ark of refuge for the Vallenses—and now Elionor. He turned left toward the wide plains of Piedmont and the countless lands beyond. These mountains were safe and peaceful, but out there he could take part in God's eternal plan for the souls of men.

He slid the box back into his pocket and walked down the ridge to a world that needed him.

Acknowledgments

Though *The Outcast of Chivasso* is shorter than my two previous books, I am still deeply thankful for all the help and encouragement.

A few days after I finished the first draft, I asked my wife and four children if they wanted to listen to me read the not-yet-titled story. Those five evenings we gathered in the living room were some of my favorite memories of the year. My family patiently listened, even as I paused to take notes about their reaction or a change I needed to make. Without a doubt, Andrea and my four children—Allen, Eric, Aliza, and Emma—brought emotion and depth to characters like Raimond, Elionor, Damiano, and even Norma.

Diana Wilbur, Vonda Murdock, Jenna Starr, and Truman Henricks were the early readers I needed. Their varied perspectives brought further depth to the story, including the immortèla flowers and Damiano's spiritual progression.

The process of editing a story, no matter the length, is an arduous but necessary process. Jayna Baas is meticulous, direct, and creative in her own right. I deeply value her advice and trust her knowledge of both storytelling and language.

Life stories, both real and imagined, were tremendous inspirations to *The Outcast of Chivasso*. Cherished nineteenth-century authors ranging from Dickens to Hugo to Dostoevsky depicted both the downtrodden and the oppressors in their renowned works. Those established archetypes allowed me to build upon foundations that have already been perfected.

I continue to be amazed and humbled by those who read what I write. Some readers finish a book in a day, while others take a year. Either way, reading is a choice, and for those who choose to read something from me—thank you.

I claim no talent of myself and no ability to write outside the Lord, and it's for Him first I write. He is an Advocate for outcasts, a Comforter for grieving hearts, and a Savior for sinful souls.

Historical Notes

The Outcast of Chivasso is set in 1445, about fourteen years before the events in *Heretics of Piedmont*. The historical scope of this book was smaller in scale than *Heretics of Piedmont* or *The Lord of Luserna*, but it necessitated some unique research into subjects like wintertime hygiene in the Late Middle Ages, the fifteenth-century concept of adoption, and the Crusade of Varna.

All characters in this book are fictional, but Raimond Durand is a cross section of the Waldensian barbes who secretly traveled throughout Europe in this era. The fog of time has shrouded their lives and work, and what we do know about them often comes from those who sought their demise. Some facts about them, however, have been generally established. Barbes usually traveled in pairs, though not always. Also, they trained in other professions, such as medicine or masonry, to conceal their true work.

The village of Chivasso (pronounced *kee-VAH-so*) sits on the Po River about twelve miles northeast of Turin, Italy; in the late fifteenth century, it was known by its Piedmontese name, Civass. The cathedral mentioned in this book, Chiesa Collegiata di Santa Maria Assunta, still stands in the village square.

The Outcast of Chivasso features the two common languages of medieval Piedmont. The Piedmontese language is still spoken, though its use has slowly dwindled. I took advantage of modern lexicons to adapt the few Piedmontese phrases and idioms in this text. Waldensians like Raimond, Lambert, and Magdalena would have spoken Old Occitan (*Romaunt* in this story) which is related to Piedmontese but distinct enough to make mutual intelligibility most likely difficult. Because Latin was the primary language of business, literature, and church records in the Middle Ages, Piedmontese and Old Occitan were rarely written; because of that, the fifteenth-century state of these languages is impossible to fully understand. For that reason, I took some liberty by leaning on the modern state of these languages.

All Bible quotations are from the King James Version. Of course, that translation did not exist in the 1400s, but I thought it best to use a version most readers would be familiar with rather than translating the verses myself. For this story, I feel the King James Version offers a sense of antiquity without losing scriptural intelligibility, familiarity, and accuracy.

The campaign in which Damiano and Vilfred fought is known as the Crusade of Varna. Though the crusaders were initially successful, the Ottomans decisively turned them back in 1444 in the Battle of Varna. This marked the beginning of Ottoman supremacy that would endure for at least two more centuries. The crusade was mostly carried out by Poland, Hungary, and other Eastern European kingdoms, but there were contingents from the Papal States and other Western European powers; Damiano and Vilfred would have been in that group.

Legal matters in the medieval world are a fascinating subject, especially in the rare cases of adoption. Would Vilfred's final wishes have been honored? A question like this depended on the current whims of the local magistrates, clergy, and nobility. Adoption as we know it today was seldom a legal matter then; a relative or friend would have typically taken in a child if her parents died, but in Elionor's unique scenario, other factors would have come into play. With the resources at my disposal, I tried to offer a plausible and historically accurate outcome that reflected both the Waldensians' reputation of compassion as well as the legal ramifications of a perceived heretic assuming guardianship of a Catholic orphan.

Overall, *The Outcast of Chivasso* is a fictional story but one I strived to convey accurately, believably, and engagingly.

Selected Bibliography

Allix, Pierre. Some Remarks Upon the Ecclesiastical History of the Ancient Churches of Piedmont. United Kingdom: Clarendon Press, 1821.

Audisio, Gabriel. Preachers by Night: The Waldensian Barbes (15th–16th Centuries). Netherlands: Brill, 2006.

Beattie, William. The Waldenses: Or, Protestant Valleys of Piedmont, Dauphiny, and the Ban de la Roche. United Kingdom: George Virtue, 1838.

Dormandy, John. A History of Savoy: Gatekeeper of the Alps. United Kingdom: Fonthill Media, 2018.

Gallenga, Antonio Carlo Napoleone. History of Piedmont. United Kingdom: Chapman and Hall, 1855.

Henderson, Ebenezer. The Vaudois: Observations Made During a Tour to the Valleys of Piedmont. United Kingdom: John Snow, Paternoster Row, 1845.

Jones, William. The History of the Christian Church from the Birth of Christ to the Xviii. Century. United States: R.W. Pomeroy, 1832.

Lacroix, Paul. Manners, Customs, and Dress During the Middle Ages, and During the Renaissance Period. United Kingdom: Chapman and Hall, 1876.

Morland, Samuel. The History of the Evangelical Churches of the Valleys of Piemont. United Kingdom: Henry Hills, one of His Highness's printers, 1658.

Muston, Alexis. The Israel of the Alps: A History of the Persecutions of the Waldenses. United Kingdom: Ingram, Cooke, 1852.

Wylie, James Aitken. The History of Protestantism. United Kingdom: Cassel, Petter & Galpin, 1874.

ABOUT THE AUTHOR

D. J. Speckhals is the author of Witnesses of the Light, a historical fiction series set in the fifteenth century featuring the Waldensians.

Since he was a young boy, Dustin has been passionate about history and geography. He spent many school nights up late studying National Geographic and Rand McNally atlases trying to capture a glimpse of the world outside his home in Michigan. After receiving his B.A. in Pastoral Theology in 2009, he married Andrea and moved to southeast Pennsylvania, where he has made his career as a software developer.

Other than writing, Dustin enjoys serving in various ministries in his local church, running, critiquing pizza, and going on adventures with his wife and their four kids.

www.djspeckhals.com
Facebook: @DJSpeckhals
Instagram: @d.j.speckhals

If you loved this book, please give it a review online. Positive reviews help so much. Thank you.

If you loved *The Outcast of Chivasso*, There's more!

Few oppose the Roman Church's domination.
A monk spies on rebels hiding in the mountains.
Will he destroy the rebels or embrace them?

They've discovered an ancient Bible.
Now a tyrant seeks to destroy it.
Can they release it to its glorious liberty?
Or will they burn along with it?